Focus On

Edited by Gail Thornhill

Table of Contents

Preface

Focus On is my first work of fiction and an attempt to learn more and share with others about ADHD, Attention Deficit Hyperactivity Disorder. I know several people affected by it but didn't feel compelled to read a clinical explanation. Yet writing a fictional account of a young woman struggling with it sounded fun. (My definition of fun is often different than the rest of the world.) And it worked. I enjoyed doing the research along the way and learned a ton. The early readers of my book said the same.

I'll start here with a quick definition. According to the Cleveland Clinic, *ADHD is a neurodevelopmental disorder which affects how your brain develops. Symptoms begin before age 12 and include fidgeting, difficulty paying attention and losing things. ADHD is treatable with medications and therapies that manage symptoms and make daily life easier.*

As the title suggests, ADHD is a challenge of focus. People with ADHD sometimes seem to have multiple threads of thought happening at the same time. Interestingly, people with ADHD can also go into a mode of hyperfocus. They will find something of interest to them, like Sophia will with her coffee research and lose track of everything else around her.

But wait. I don't want to give away too much yet. You can read on to learn more as our main characters move through their own ADHD journey. Regardless of what you know or not about ADHD, I hope you learn something and enjoy reading this book!

Chapter 1

"Earth to Sophia, come in, Sophia." I startled back to the moment to find my coworker, Ethan standing over my cubicle with a concerned look on his face.

"Thought we'd lost you for a minute," says Ethan. "Sorry, Ethan. I was just thinking about a few things."

Well, more than a few things. I was lost in so many thoughts I couldn't keep them all straight…the project I was behind on, the conversation I had last week with my supervisor, the gas bill that was overdue, what I wanted to make for dinner…and more.

"Do you want to grab coffee and chat?" Ethan's warm smile and tiny dimple in his left cheek helped ease me off the ledge of anxiety I had been walking for the last few minutes. Or was it longer than a few minutes?

Ethan offered a boyish grin. His grayish green eyes looked warm and inviting.

"Sure, but where should we go? The coffee at the diner is almost passable, but that place is always so packed, even in the off season."

We leave our workplace, a boring three story corporate looking building at the edge of downtown Lyndville, Virginia. Downtown would be a generous description of the small center of the city. Most of the downtown area had been built in the

1940s and consisted of quaint brick buildings housing shops that supported the thriving tourism industry. A mile to the east was the Atlantic Ocean. Each year, the city population swelled to three times its normal size from early June through the end of August. Guests renting cottages, condos, and hotels flocked to the grocery store, the souvenir shop, the beach rental kiosk, and the diner. Locals appreciated the tourists for supporting their livelihood and yet got tired of how busy the traffic and businesses got each year through the summer months.

The streets were relatively quiet at 10AM and we walked along in companionable silence. The temperature was comfortable in September, not too hot and not too cold.

Once we arrived at the diner and got our coffee, Ethan gave me that concerned look again and said, "Spill, Sophia, what's the matter?"

Tears that had been threatening finally came pouring out, along with a few minutes of wracking sobs. Ethan hugged me and let me cry it out, patting my back, stroking my hair and murmuring quiet words of encouragement.

"OK, I didn't mean spill *that* literally, Blanchard".

I chuckle in spite of myself and take a deep breath.

"Well…last week when I had my performance review, I got a "does not meet" rating and Jean told me I'm on performance improvement. I missed due dates for three major project deliverables and the other team members are complaining. I don't know what's wrong with me but I'm having a hard time focusing long enough to get my work done. I'm always getting texts and messages and emails that take me away from the real work they pay me to do. I get pulled into meetings that don't matter and then have a hard time getting re-started on the work."

I sigh and take another deep breath. "Thanks for listening, just saying that out loud takes a weight off my shoulders. I haven't told anyone else what's going on."

My current project is for a coffee bean producer who is revamping their product line up. My job is to help them revise their website to have a more modern look and feel and highlight the new products in a way that will increase sales of the most profitable coffees. This company gives a portion of their profits back to support ethical production of coffee beans. I'll also figure out how to highlight those facts; fair payment to the workers and minimal environmental impact.

Ethan gives me another hug and pauses, appearing to be lost in thought for a moment.

"Sophia, that super sucks. I can relate. It's a wonder any of us ever get any work done these days with the number of interruptions that come along every day, hell, every minute and every second. I've had my own challenges with my work performance and found out about three years ago that I have ADHD, Attention Deficit Hyperactivity Disorder. I'm not saying that's what you have and even if you did, my experience with it may or may not be the same. But it was such a relief when I figured out what was going on and then started to do something about it."

"Oh, wow, Ethan, that blows! What's it been like?"

"Don't be sorry. It's just like any other human characteristic, physical or mental. We all have some things going for us and against us. I, for one, am devastatingly handsome and charming, but I missed out when they were passing out the focus genes. I thought they said "f★ us" so I skipped the line."

I burst out laughing and punch Ethan's muscled shoulder. "I mean I've heard of ADHD, but I always thought it was something only 10 year old boys got and they eventually grew out of it."

"What we know about ADHD comes largely from dealing with 10-year-old boys, probably because they make the most trouble at home and in the classroom. In my simple understanding, I have a deficiency in my brain wiring. Mine 'short circuit' sometimes. I have a hard time focusing on things that aren't interesting to me...that's the attention deficit part. Plus I can get fidgety and impulsive...that's the hyperactivity part. And with ADHD, sometimes my short circuits can cause emotional volatility because my brain regions aren't communicating well. You know, left hand doesn't know what right hand is doing.

"Again, not saying that's what you have, just saying for me, figuring out what was going on, understanding what I can do about it and giving myself a break was a huge relief. I no longer think I'm broken, just that I have a different brain structure that screws up sometimes. My situation is no different than someone who has a heart murmur…one of my organs has the hiccups, so I need to know that and handle it appropriately."

Now it's my turn to give Ethan a hug. "Thanks for sharing. I had no idea you were going through that."

"Enough about me, tell me about your performance review."

I groan. "Aghhhh, I knew I had missed some deadlines but to hear Jean describe it, my misses were big issues to the rest of the team. So much so, the team whined to them about it. I know we have deadlines and due dates but someone is always dragging me into a meeting, texting me, and messaging me to where I feel like I can't get anything done! But Jean considered those excuses and basically told me I need to shape up or ship out. I'm on a "performance plan", so I have to meet with Jean weekly and go through my work and basically get my ass handed to me if I'm still missing deadlines. And oh, by the way, I have a life outside of work. I have bills to pay, appliances that break, friends and family to support. I'm not going to work a million hours like Jean does. Speaking of Jean, did you know the actress who is also named Jean who played the psychiatrist in Oppenheimer was also in "Black Widow?"

"No way! I know that movie was supposed to be so great, but I could never get past the darkness and watch it all the way through…"

We continue to discuss movies and drink coffee for another hour. I enjoy Ethan's company and he's handsome in a boy next door kind of way. He's fit but not overly muscular and he has golden brown hair that is a few shades lighter than mine in color with gentle waves. His skin is clear, while I have a few freckles on my nose and cheeks.

"Well, we should get back to the ranch…also known as the office. Let me know if you ever want to talk again or if I can do anything to help you," says Ethan.

"Thank you, I will," I say.

Chapter 2

I'm going to be late for work…again. In my rush to get groceries put away, laundry done, garbage to the curb, and all the other tasks of the night, I misplaced my car keys. I look in all the usual places I normally put my keys but no luck. I take a deep, calming breath and start over. Where in the world would they be?

After another 15 minutes of searching my apartment, I found my keys on top of the cluttered dryer, half hidden under a sock. I must have set them there when I pulled out the laundry. I throw my hands up in exasperation.

On my drive to work I call Jean. "Jean, I wanted to let you know I'm running late today." On the other end of the line, silence. Jean sighs and says, "Sophia, the whole team is waiting for you to start the meeting. We'll go ahead and you'll need to catch up. I don't think I need to tell you this does not look good on your performance plan."

"I'm truly sorry, and this won't…" I was about to say it won't happen again but it doesn't ring true. "This won't impact the team, I'll make sure of it by catching up with them afterwards."

Jean sighs deeply. "Sophia, this does affect the team because they have to spend extra time with you rehashing what was discussed." Jean is right, but there's nothing else I can do right now to make it better.

On the drive to work my anxiety ratchets up. I try to distract my thinking by fantasizing about quitting. That'll show them. I would march into the meeting and announce to the whole team, "You all will have to figure out how to do this project without me because I won the lottery. So…so there!"

But reality sets in. With bills to pay and minimal savings in the bank, quitting is not an option for me at the moment. And in a town as small as Lyndville, good jobs are hard to come by. The company I work for, Cloudscape, pays well and is one of the few large companies that hire people in my profession as a product manager. And I actually like the work.

As I think about how I'll structure the website as I drive, I almost miss the turn into the parking garage. How in the world can that happen when I drive this way five days a week? I've now missed almost half the meeting and I rush through the garage, into the building and to the gray conference room.

The whole team turns when I walk in and most give me an annoyed look. Jean keeps their face neutral and Ethan gives me a supportive smile and nod. I decide an apology is the best route. "I am soooo sorry for my tardiness. I had an issue with my car," which is mostly true. "Please continue and I'll catch up."

"Well, we haven't gotten very far, Sophia, because we need your input on the highest priority features for the next iteration," Chris, one of the developers, explains.

"Yes, understood, I think we should work on the highlights page for their farming practices. I'll have some mockups ready by the end of the day. Does that work?" Chris gives a thumbs up and the team continues to walk through their progress and issues.

I hurry back to my tan cubicle, determined to meet the commitment I just made to the team. I start working on the website design until my phone rings...

"Hi, Mom, what's up?" My mom sounds panicked. "Do you remember where I put the paperwork for your dad's upcoming hospital stay? I need to fill it out and turn it in by the end of today or his surgery will have to be postponed."

I picture my parents' house, with dusty piles of stuff on tables and chairs and overflowing shelves. "No, Mom, sorry I don't. Did you look in the extra bedroom filing drawers? I thought you said you were going to centralize the papers there."

"Yes, that was the plan, but I just didn't get around to it yet. I didn't mean to bother you at work. I'll find it. Hey, did you see the episode of Bridgerton yet whe-?"

I cut my mom off. "Mom, I do need to get back to work; call me back if you can't find it in a few hours."

I make slow but steady progress in the next hour. Then I attend another team meeting, a United Way campaign meeting, and I get called into an urgent production meeting. As I head back to my desk, I start to panic about the lack of progress I've made this morning. I'm probably about 10% done and the day is more than 50% over.

Before my anxiety can go into full blown mode, I stop by Ethan's cube and ask him if he wants to go to lunch. As he looks up from his screen, a lock of his golden-brown hair falls over his eye. I have a strong urge to comb it back into place. Ethan's greenish gray eyes search mine for a minute. "You ok?" he asks. "Sort of…nothing a good croissant sandwich won't set right. Oh wait, we don't have anywhere to get good croissants in this town."

We walk briskly to the diner for a quick lunch of hamburgers and french fries. As we walk I recap my conversation with Jean, the first meeting of the day, and my growing panic about the work I have yet to do today. "None of this is my fault," I whine. "I keep getting pulled away and distracted." I can feel tears threatening in the corners of my eyes.

Ethan nods thoughtfully and lets me ramble. Finally, when I stop, he replies, "Sophia, you need to say no, nicely, silence your phone and do some heavy lifting today."

"I know, you're right." I sigh and shoot him a small smile. "Thanks for letting me vent."

Once we get back to the office my head is clearer from the walk and talk with Ethan. I continue to make progress for another hour but my phone rings again. It's my mom and I can't very well ignore her; this is probably a call for help.

"Sophia, I have turned this place upside down and I still can't find your father's paperwork." I sigh and start to shut down my laptop. I decide I need to help my mom, and I can work on the website after that from home, where I won't be distracted. "I'll be over in 15 minutes."

I stop at Jean's cubicle on the way out and fill them in on the day and my plan to finish up tonight. Jean looks disappointed but says, "Well, you have to do what's right for the family. Good luck with that paperwork."

When I arrive at my parents' home, my mom's honey brown eyes, so like my own, light up and she gives me a big hug. Like me, she's fit from gardening and I can feel her strength in the hug. "I can't tell you how much I appreciate your help!"

We head into my childhood home to start the search.

Chapter 3

I hug my dad who is reclining on a brown leather chair in the sunroom. I have to maneuver around piles of yellowed newspaper, stacks of cardboard boxes containing fishing magazines, an old sewing machine, and my dad's medical equipment to reach him.

"How are you feeling today?" I ask.

"Not too bad. The doc put me on a different medicine for my indigestion and it seems to be working much better. I thought I was going to have to give up a lot of my favorite foods that have high acid content if I didn't get relief from this medicine."

My dad's medical problems are various and complicated. At 65 years old, most are typical, but he's scheduled for an upcoming surgery to have a lump removed from his shoulder. The procedure itself is straightforward but due to his age, they are taking extra precautions to be sure he's thoroughly tested before the surgery for liver function and so on.

"Thanks for coming in to help Mom with finding that paperwork for the lab workup. You know how hard it is to get into doctors and hospitals these days. I don't want to miss this chance to take care of the lump."

We get started on the hunt.

"Where have you already checked?" I ask Mom.

My mom replays the search of all usual spots: her inbox on the desk, the filing cabinet in their bedroom, the tall pile of mail on the crowded counter. Just to be safe I double check each of those piles. Each has a mix of paperwork from bank statements to bills to ads for painting companies. I don't find it surprising that my parents can't find things when the paperwork is all jumbled together as it is.

"What day did you get the paperwork and what was going on that day?" I ask.

"Well, that was the day the hot water heater broke. Tuesday, I think. We had Dad's appointment in the morning at the clinic over on the east side of town and the repair crew came over in the afternoon. We had ham salad for lunch, you know, to use up the leftover ham from the brunch this past weekend. I'm not sure why any of that would be relevant though..."

"Have you looked in the basement near the water heater? Or did you get anything from the basement to make the ham salad, like a new jar of mayo?" I ask.

"Well...no, but now I see what you're suggesting. While the basement would be a strange place to put that paperwork, if I had it in my hands when the hot water repair crew came over..."

"Exactly! Let's go look."

We look behind and around the hot water heater to no avail. We then retrace the places my mom already looked. An hour later, we're still no closer to tracking down the paperwork.

"Why don't you contact the insurance company and have them resend it?"

"Yes, that's probably best. Thanks for trying to help," Mom replies.

I *really* need to get back on my laptop and work more on website design. I head back to my apartment and fire up my computer. It's already 4:30 and my energy is starting to flag. I pull out my favorite wine glass from the cabinet and a bottle of Chardonnay before sinking tiredly into my office chair.

Thirty minutes later, I've gotten started…barely…when the phone rings. It's my mom again.

"Guess what! I found the paperwork!"

"Yayyy! Where was it?"

"It was on top of the dryer! When we were downstairs with the hot water repair crew, I grabbed the laundry and must have set it down there. We didn't see it because it was behind the extra detergent and bleach bottles."

I chuckle and tell my mom the story of my own car keys location earlier that day.

"Like mother, like daughter. From now on, maybe the laundry area should be the first place we look when we can't find something. By the way, have you watched Schitt's Creek?"

My mom goes on to tell me all about the actors, the storyline, and so on.

By the time I get started again on the website design, it's after six. I put in another hour, but my energy level continues to drop. I'm not done but part way will have to be enough, I think. Time for dinner and relaxing before bed.

Despite my passion for the coffee website, I know on some level that my personal issues and distractions sometimes get in the way. My parents mean the world to me and I'm glad to help. But my gut churns when I think about my lack of progress at work because of the time I spent at my parents' house and on the phone with my mom today.

Chapter 4

The next week, Ethan and I are having lunch together and chatting about our hopes and dreams for the future.

"Sophia, what would you do if you won the lottery? You know tonight's winnings are $100 million. I bought a ticket and I don't expect to win, but I like to imagine what I would do with my life if money were no object."

"You know, I don't think I've ever told anyone this, but there is something I've always dreamed of doing, Ethan. I want to open a coffee shop. A place where people can come and enjoy scrumptious coffee and books by the beach. Maybe I would offer some food too, flaky pastries and yummy sandwiches. But I don't know where I would even start. Planning something like that sounds so overwhelming to me."

My unease from the prior day pops into my mind and I blow out a long breath.

"Maybe I'll lose my job and that will be the wake up call I need to get started. Behind every cloud is a silver lining and all that jazz."

Ethan's eyes light up with excitement. "That's an amazing idea, Sophia! And you wouldn't have to do it alone. I could help you with the planning. We could make this dream a reality together."

Ethan got a goofy grin on his face and looked up as though he was observing his own thoughts. His eyebrows rose and he was quiet for a beat.

"Earth to Ethan!" I sang out and chuckled.

"So sorry, I went off in my own world. Even though you were in it, and I was thinking about good restaurants…never mind. So, we were talking about this coffee shop idea. Tell me more."

I wondered what he had been thinking about. Maybe he'll tell me another time.

My eyes sparkled with enthusiasm as I described a cozy, beach-themed coffee shop with comfy teal and beige striped chairs, ocean views, and shelves filled with my favorite novels. Maybe I would offer some bakery products like cinnamon rolls, muffins and fresh sandwiches, purchased locally from neighboring establishments.

Ethan listened and nodded along as I described my vision.

"Sounds great, Sophia, and I really think this town is ripe for a business like that. Have you started a business plan yet?"

My face fell. "A business plan, no…this is all just pie in the sky ideas. I never thought I could make it work. It was just a daydream of mine."

"Why not, Sophia, make lemonade out of lemons and all that? I've never done anything quite like this, but it could be fun! We could research other coffee shops, look into small business loans, and scout out locations."

I started to panic as Ethan talked more about the work needed to start a business.

"I'm more of an idea person…all of that sounds so daunting!"

"Well, why don't we get together after work one day and get started? It won't be so bad if we break it down and decide what we need to do next. I used to SUCK at this type of planning but I'm slowly learning to do it, now that I understand that my ADHD makes this difficult. But it's NOT impossible, I can show you some hacks for this type of work that have helped me."

"Let me know what night works to get started."

"I'll think about it," I reply. "But now it's your turn, Ethan, what would you do if you win the lottery tonight?

"You're the one with the ticket and all."

"Well, this is something I also have not talked to anyone else about and it would cost so much money to start. But since the winnings are $100 million, I could probably swing it once my numbers are drawn."

"I'd like to open a cat shelter. We have the main humane society on the west side of town but they handle both dogs and cats. I think it would be stressful for cats to listen to all of the dogs barking. I think cats can make great emotional support animals and I would help clients who need them get their pets. I could also help with the paperwork they need for an apartment or a workplace to certify them. I might take the cats out to the senior center to visit. For a lot of seniors, they probably had cats at home during their lifetime but can't have them at the center due to allergies and so on."

"Wow, Ethan, sounds like you've daydreamed about this a lot.

"And I also think you have a fantastic idea here. How about your business plan?"

Ethan's eyes narrow.

"Touche, Sophia, that's a fair question and no, I haven't started my business plan for my cat shelter. Maybe once I win the lottery, I'll get more serious about it. For now, we should probably get back to work at our real jobs."

Chapter 5

The following Thursday after work, Ethan and I get together at the park by the beach for a picnic and planning party. Ethan had suggested we call it that to avoid thinking of it as a daunting chore...no, it's a super fun party! The sound of the waves worked its magic to put me in a calm mood right away.

"Before we start the party," I say hesitantly, "can you tell me more about your experience with ADHD?" I think I might have it too, and hearing about how you're handling it may be helpful.

"Well be careful, Sophia, because my experience is just that, mine. You may have ADHD but not the same symptoms to the same degree. Just like any other disease, mileage may vary. Think about all the different types of cancers people can have, how serious they are, and how they are treated. SUPER different across the board.

"But there are two basic types with similar symptoms. With the hyperactive type, a person likely talks a lot, fidgets, and interrupts others. It's hard for them to wait their turn, and they may speak at inappropriate times. People with the inattentive type have a tough time organizing or finishing tasks, paying attention to details, and are easily distracted.

"And some people have a combination of these symptoms, a double whammy so to speak. Also, a diagnosis can be tricky because these symptoms may only show occasionally or be caused by some other issue. So, is it ADHD, anxiety or just tiredness?"

I nod. This is all sounding so familiar. I decide to do some googling on my own to learn more.

"Anyway, the important thing for any of us with ADHD or any of these symptoms, honestly, is to accept them and figure out how to best manage and treat them. ADHD is generally treated with therapy and sometimes medications.

"Through therapy I've learned about creating routines, putting things away in the same place all the time, limiting choices, and breaking down tasks into smaller, more manageable chunks.

"Also, I like to reward myself when I do something that's hard for me with my ADHD. For example, I had a closet that needed cleaning out and I told myself once I finished that, I would go out for ice cream. I have to say, I had an awful time with that and found every distraction known to humans to avoid doing it. But eventually, I really wanted my ice cream, so I set aside an hour a day for three days to work on it, set a timer and guess what? I did it! It's also a reward in and of itself to be able to see what I have in there and not have to search so hard to find my ice skates and scarves."

"Wow, a lot of what you just said really resonates with me. Especially the…what did you call it, inattentive form? I feel like my brain sometimes short circuits when I start laundry at the beginning of the day and find it the next day, soaking wet. I could have sworn I finished that task! But my smelly clothes that need to be re-washed tell me otherwise."

"So, what type do you have and how else are you treating it?" I ask.

"I'm a combo platter so I get double the fun in managing my ADHD. I've been in therapy for a couple years now and am still learning what strategies I need to put in place to keep my sh★t together. Therapists can make all kinds of helpful suggestions like 'set reminders' but if I ignore said reminders because I'm too caught up in something else, or I just don't see it because I get distracted by texts and Instagram notifications and…you get it. And for me, a lot of the time the reminders are to do boring stuff that I don't like to do. So it's difficult to do them because my brain is low on dopamine already and boring stuff doesn't give me the enjoyment I crave."

"Dopa what? That sounds like a good name for a band."

"Dopamine. People with ADHD have unique gene characteristics that make it difficult for our brains to respond to dopamine. It helps us with attention and feelings of pleasure. Medically speaking, they talk about defective genes but I just like to call it unique."

"Wow, interesting. So maybe the band name should be Defective Gene and the Dopamines…and the lead singer will be named Gene, at least their stage name," I joke.

Ethan seems to miss my feeble attempt at humor and continues.

"I'm not sure if I'll get this exactly right, but if one person in a family is diagnosed with ADHD, it's something like nine times more likely for them to have a close relative who also has it. I could go on and on about it, I find the subject so interesting. But for now, let's save that thought. Let's get back to the coffee shop plan at hand."

Later that day, I did some research and found excellent resources on ADHD. And the more I read, the more I wondered if I had it too.

Resources
CDC ADHD Overview
https://www.cdc.gov/adhd/index.html

Understood AHDH Overview
https://www.understood.org/en/adhd

Chapter 6

Ethan and I start to outline the business plan. We find artificial intelligence business plan generators and examples online of other plans to get a quick start. My excitement grows as we fill in the templates. There doesn't seem to be much competition for a coffee shop in our little town and the demand, especially in the summer, is huge.

When we get to the section on "what will set you apart and why will customers buy from you", I giggle. "Should I write down something sassy here like, "to avoid being poisoned by the diner coffee?"

Ethan's eyes twinkle with amusement. "I'd tone it down a little. After all, the bank you'll be asking for a loan may not have that much of a sense of humor. Of course, if they've had the diner coffee, they may be inclined to agree."

Ethan seems to be studying my face while we're working on the business plan.

I can feel myself blushing and I turn my head.

Although Ethan has been a wonderful friend throughout my recent work issues, I don't think of him "that way". Besides, dating someone with ADHD would probably make things difficult in a relationship. And I'm not sure dating a co-worker would be a good idea. And what if we decided to go into business together in the coffee shop? That could become really awkward. And maybe I'm just imagining that Ethan has any feelings for me. It's not as though he has ever asked me out for anything other than casual work outings or to work on this business plan.

I try to focus back on the task at hand. We've made good progress but have lots of the template left to complete. When we get to the section on financial data, my enthusiasm starts to wane. I never liked math anyway, let alone thinking about accounting and financial modeling.

"A cash flow statement?!?!? I don't have any cash flow, that's the whole problem," I say, partly joking and partly serious.

"Well you have to figure out where you'll get enough cash to at least start up and pay salaries and rent, buy the coffee inventory and so on when you're getting started. If you don't have all of that outlined, you'll never get a loan from a bank," Ethan patiently explains.

"And equipment. I have to figure out what I need and how much all of that will cost. Do you know of any cheap places where I can get an industrial espresso maker and dishwasher? Maybe I'll start looking on TikTok Shop," I joke.

"Let's talk more about location, I'd like your opinion. Plus, that sounds way more fun."

"Do you think closer to the beach or closer to the business district would be a better bet?" I ask.

"Well, that depends on how many customers you expect to have during the tourist season vs. throughout the year. If you project that out, it might give you a better answer to that question. It seems like the business district would give you a more stable stream of revenue to pay the bills throughout the year. But you should make some projections and mock up what that might do to your sales numbers."

"Ewwww, I know you're right on track, but that sounds tough to do. If I wanted to locate on the beach, maybe I could even make it a food truck type set up so I could move it around based on where the action is. And maybe I could even move it to the business district in the non-tourist season," I say.

"I like that idea. You'll need to look into the zoning laws and figure out what the city allows that way, but it could really be a benefit to maximizing your revenue and giving yourself flexibility throughout the year. And if you still wanted to set up some tables and chairs outside to make it a café type experience, you can factor in portability when you're buying the furniture. On the flip side, that does make it more dependent on the weather. Most people wouldn't want to hang out outside on a rainy day, and of course it does get pretty cold around here in the late fall and winter months," Ethan replies.

"Zoning laws, yeah, wonder where in the world I would track those down. And the weather; I wonder how many days a year we get that are not raining and a decent enough temperature to make outdoor seating attractive. Aghhh, this is sooooo hard. I'm running out of steam here."

I sigh. While I'm super excited about this idea, these details give me a headache.

"I appreciate your help but I need to take a break from this. Can we pick up another time?" I ask.

"Of course. When would you like to get together again?" Ethan asks.

"Well, my dad has his surgery this week, so it will have to be next week. Or maybe even two weeks out," I answer.

Ethan and I make a plan to get together the following Tuesday.

"Can I give you a ride home?" Ethan asks.

"No thanks, I think I'll walk. I need the quiet time to let my brain process all of this." I say. Inwardly, I'm also thinking I shouldn't be leading Ethan on when I've got so much else going on in my life right now.

Ethan's shoulders slump. A look of disappointment flickers on his face. I wonder for a minute if he was about to ask me out. Or does he feel rejected, as though I want to get away from him sooner rather than later? I want him to know how much I appreciate his help, but I really do just need to walk and think. My head is spinning.

"Well, I'll see you next week then, have a nice rest of your evening," Ethan responds.

"Ethan, thank you SOOOOOO much for your help with this. You're so knowledgeable, and I truly appreciate all of your insights and your patience. I'll see you next week."

Chapter 7

The next few days pass in a blur. My dad's surgery takes up the whole day because I insist on driving my parents to the hospital, staying through the procedure, and taking them home.

While we wait in the boring, beige waiting room, my mom and I pass the time reading and chatting about this and that. My recent challenges at work and the conversations I've been having with Ethan come to mind.

"Mom, did I ever tell you about my daydream of opening a coffee shop?"

"No, honey, you didn't but I think that would be a wonderful thing. Lord knows this town is a coffee desert!

"And the tourists in the summer months would bring a huge influx of business and income."

"Yeah, that's what I think too. And I'm thinking about selling books and maybe some food. You know, not having a full-blown kitchen but buying from some of the other businesses. And buying the books second hand from libraries and such, mostly so they don't go into landfills."

"Wow, honey, you've thought a lot about this. Are you really going to do it?"

I sigh. "I'd love to but it takes money to get started, obviously. I have a friend at work who's helping me start a business plan. And it's REALLY HARD for me to keep focused on that with everything else going on."

My mom looks at me closely. "What else, besides your dad's surgery, do you mean?"

I tell my mom about being on performance improvement and how difficult it has been for me to handle the day-to-day priorities.

"Oh, Sophia, I'm so sorry to hear that. Is there anything I can do?"

"Nothing I can think of, other than win the lottery. Say, do you happen to have a couple hundred thousand bucks sitting around? Then I can just leave my job and open this coffee shop like I'd like."

"I'll go buy a lottery ticket today," she quips.

"And did you ever have trouble like I'm having at work?"

"No, I can't say I have but you may want to ask your dad when he's feeling better. I seem to recall him having some rocky times during the time he was working for Lyndville Insurance.

Thankfully, the surgery goes well. A few days later, when my dad is mostly recovered, I head into the sunroom to ask him about it. He looks comfy in his worn, brown chair.

"Dad, I don't know if Mom told you but I'm having some trouble at work. I've missed some deadlines, and my boss put me on performance improvement. It's kind of three strikes and you're out type thing. I like my job and I'm pretty good at it, but I get so distracted sometimes and have a hard time finishing deliverables on time. Since I work on a team, it's a big deal because it can slow everything down."

Dad looks at me with concern. "Oh, Sophia, Mom didn't mention it, and I'm sorry to hear that. I went through something similar early in my career at the insurance company. I wasn't meeting the sales metrics in the trial portion of my contract. My boss told me I should quit and that I wasn't cut out to be in that job. It isn't exactly what you're dealing with, but anything like that can be a blow to your confidence, especially coming from your boss."

"Why do you suppose you weren't meeting the sales metrics?" I ask.

"Well, I had a lot on my mind with running a new business and having a family. Sales was a priority, but so was hiring staff, renting a place, buying supplies. And oh, by the way, Mom was pregnant with you so I wanted to be there for her at least some of the time. I wanted to have a life not just a job ,and that isn't easy for most of us. What's that famous quote? *Never get so busy making a living that you forget to make a life.*"

"Oh wow, I love that, who said that?"

"Dolly Parton" Dad chuckles. "And can you imagine how hard it would be for someone like Dolly to have a life, what with all of the commitments she would have on her plate?"

"So what happened with your boss and your job?"

"I was on probation for several months and had to meet with the boss to review the metrics every two weeks. Over time, I figured out I was really good at running the business, the operational stuff but not such a good salesperson. So, I hired someone else to do most of the heavy lifting in sales while I made sure our office ran smoothly and we were profitable. I have a pretty good head for numbers, so the key was to sell the right stuff to the right clients, not just sell lots of policies. I used that to show my boss the metrics he was using didn't tell the whole story and eventually, he got off my back."

"That's awesome, Dad, I never knew you went through that."

"*What doesn't kill you makes you stronger,*" her dad responds.

"Oh Dad, you and your quotes." Who said that? "I thought Kelly Clarkson came up with that in her song."

"Nietzsche, a German philosopher first used that phrase, way back in 1888."

"Good to hear, Dad, good to know. Both Kelly Clarkson and Nietzsche are so right."

Chapter 8

The following Tuesday as I hurried down the street, I collided with a man carrying a pair of binoculars. Books flew out of my bag, scattering across the sandy sidewalk.

"Oh no, I'm so sorry!" I say while kneeling down to gather my fallen books.

The man bent down to help me, his warm smile lighting his face. "No harm done," he said, handing me a slightly sandy copy of "The Collected Stories."

"I'm Bryan, by the way."

I looked up, meeting his kind, dark bluish gray eyes.

I noticed his wavy blackish brown hair somehow looked neat and casual at the same time. His forearms were solid muscle with a small tattoo of a scorpion on his right arm and a woodpecker on his left arm.

"Sophia," I replied, taking the book from him. "Thank you."

Over the next few hours, I couldn't stop thinking about Bryan. His smile, his kindness, and the way he had treated me with such care. Not to mention he was downright handsome in a classic sense of the word. I wondered why he had the tattoos he had chosen. I found myself wanting to return to the corner where we had met, hoping to see him again.

Fate seemed to favor me, as later that day, I found him browsing the shelves of the local bookstore. "Bryan," I called out, a smile spreading across my face.

"Sophia," he replied, turning around with a look of surprise and delight. "I was hoping I'd run into you again. Although this time, I was hoping it was less literal, I mean running into you. I hope you and your books are ok."

"Oh I'm fine, my books are fine. I was distracted while I was walking. I should know better than to get so caught up in my thoughts. I often don't pay attention to where I'm going. Anyway, I'm glad we ran into each other. You're new in town, right? I've not seen you around before and this is a pretty small town."

"Yep, I just moved here from Pittsburgh."

We spent a few minutes discussing our favorite books and sharing stories. Bryan moved to Lyndville to be closer to family. His mom's health wasn't good, and he wanted to be close to support her and his dad. He talked about Pittsburgh and how he would miss the charm of the city as well as the sports teams the city embraced. He was an avid birdwatcher and carried binoculars everywhere. As we talked, I kept sneaking glances at his face. He had a strong nose, a faint stubble of dark brown hair on his chin and full lips that I found myself staring at while he spoke, wondering what it would be like to kiss them. I knew I was jumping ahead but I could see how this attraction could blossom into something deeper.

Bryan probably noticed how my eyes would light up when I spoke about something I was passionate about, and how I sometimes struggled to focus on one thing at a time. I shared my dreams of someday opening a coffee shop and my struggles at work. I talked about my own parents' health and how I was glad to be around to help them with medical appointments. I shared how it was difficult to juggle that along with the demands of my work and of day to day living. At times, I felt as though I jumped so quickly from one topic to the next it made Bryan dizzy. Bryan nevertheless seemed to enjoy my ramblings and my unique way of seeing the world.

Bryan was in the middle of telling me a funny story from his move from Pittsburgh when he got a text that distracted him. He frowned and looked at his phone.

"I'm sorry, Sophia, but I need to go. I need to take care of something urgent."

I was disappointed to see him go and wished him well on whatever urgent matter had come up. I wondered what was going on that pulled him away so quickly without any mention of getting back together. I guessed he wasn't feeling the same way about me as I was about him.

Later that evening, Ethan and I got back together to work on the business plan at a local pub.

"How has your week been, Sophia?"

"Pretty good. My dad's surgery went very well, and you'll never guess what happened this morning." I tell Ethan about my encounter with Bryan and my sense that I could see having a relationship with him.

Ethan absorbs the news and offers me a small smile. A flicker of some emotion I can't quite read passes across his face briefly.

"That's great, Sophia. I hope everything works out."

We dive back into the business plan for another hour until I stretch and barely cover up a yawn.

"This is hard…and booooooooring! I don't know how much more of this I can take," I groan.

"How can I put together a table of milestones when I don't know when the funding will be approved? Or even if the funding will be approved?"

"You'll need to make a projection, Sophia, just 'putting it down on paper' so to speak. The bank will need to have something to react to. And you know if we don't time it right, we will miss out on the busy tourist season, which will be really important to your bottom line."

"You're right, Ethan and you're sooooo much better at this than I am. I don't think I have what it takes to do this."

Ethan raises his hand as though he was about to brush a few strands of hair away from my cheek as my chin slumps toward my chest.

"Do you mean tonight or ever?" Ethan asks with concern.

"Tonight for sure…I'll have to think about the "ever" part.

"I'm sorry I'm cutting it short tonight. It's been a long day and I have a lot on my mind. Maybe I'll be more into it again after I get some rest. I'll let you know how I feel later," I answer. My head is spinning and I barely manage a goodbye before I rush to my car.

I can feel Ethan watching me as I go. I can tell he's disappointed we're parting ways with no plans to see each other again, other than at work.

Chapter 9

I sleep fitfully that night with dreams of the coffee shop,
lustful thoughts about Bryan and then Ethan pops into my
mind...?

*I'm at the grand opening of my new café, situated right on
the beach with charming wrought iron tables with teal and
sand-colored accents all around. A sea themed mural covers the
side of one wall where the customers wait to place their orders
with a fanciful school of fish, made to look like their names.
The dogfish has a labrador head. The catfish has a calico face
with white, tan, and black spots covering its scales. Two lionfish
lounge nearby with lovely full manes and sharp teeth on a scaly
red and black body with pointy spines.*

*Bryan walks in with a bouquet of daisies and is wearing his
bathing suit with nothing else.*

*"Congratulations on your grand opening! I'd love to try
some of your goods. Can I please place an order for some of the
delicious muffins I've heard about?" He winks in a way that
suggests he means more than the pastries.*

*I can't help but notice his beautiful physique...strong biceps,
toned abs, and powerful thighs. Bryan has a tattoo across his
chest that looks like a seahorse fighting a current. I look away*

before I can spend too much time noticing what's in between all those lovely features.

Behind the counter, Ethan draws my attention by calling out, "Order up for Ollie the octopus. One lobster latte and a mussel muffin. I have a tray of clam croissants in the oven now, if Ollie is interested." He looks adorable in his chef's coat, greenish-gray eyes twinkling with excitement at the opening of the café. A flush blooms on my cheeks, having been caught by Ethan while I was ogling Bryan.

Ethan doesn't seem concerned or offended, just smiles and holds out the food tray.

I pick up the tray of food and head toward Ollie's table. But when I turn back around to deliver it, I notice Bryan has turned into a seahorse. Where his rippling abs used to be, Bryan now has a series of bony plates. His powerful thighs have turned into a curled tail.

He's no longer smiling and his seahorse face appears blank, almost menacing. The daisies have fallen to the floor since he no longer has hands or arms to hold them.

My jaw drops and I rush to pick up the flowers on the floor while my mind scrambles to understand Bryan's transition into a seahorse. And what will I say to him if he asks me out on a date?

Suddenly the clam shells over the door make the tinkling sound letting me know another customer has arrived.

In walks my boss, Jean. But Jean isn't quite Jean, Jean is part...well mostly a jellyfish. Jean smiles awkwardly, being a jellyfish and says, "Sophia, we need to talk. All of the time you're spending on this coffee shop is making your work performance even more of an issue.

"You seem distracted all the time, you're late arriving and early to leave. I'm afraid I'm going to have to..."

I burst into tears right then. I'm mortified that my emotions have gotten the best of me on today of all days.

But it's all too much...how can I do a good job at my job, open a coffee shop, and juggle two men. Wait, am I really juggling two men? I never thought of Ethan as anything but a friend. But what an understanding friend he's been. And he's so good at cooking and helped so much with starting up the café. My confusion and swirling thoughts bring on a new set of sobs.

Bryan the seahorse looks agitated and says, "I'm still waiting for my food here." He taps his tail impatiently against the counter and scowls. "You're really going to need to up your game in customer service if you want to be successful in this business."

"But you only placed your order two minutes ago and you can see there's a lot going on now, I have other customers and-"

Bryan cuts me off and says. "I'm here now and I expect white glove service. You think that stupid octopus deserves to

46

be served before me?" He huffs, and with that, he turns from a pale shade of brown to a dull green and swims out the door.

My mom appears suddenly, her mermaid tail swishing elegantly behind her. I take in the transformation of my mom's legs into a sparkling, sleek tail. It seems to make sense in the dream. My mom gives me a hug and says, "You have a lot on your plate right now. Get it, plate…cafe. Anyways, maybe some of it needs to come off. This coffee shop is a dream come true for you, and I understand how much work you've done to make it happen. I couldn't be happier for you and Ethan. This seahorse, Bryan, I'm not so sure about. He seems a little, well, arrogant. And Jean needs to pick the right time and place to have this conversation with you. I can't believe Jean said all that in front of your customers on your opening day in your shop. The more I think about it, the more I want to smack Jean with my mermaid tail. I'm only kidding of course, but really, Jean should know better. All I mean to say, Sophia, is don't worry, what is meant to be will be under the sea."

I startle awake in a sweat. All of the things on my mind had come together in a strange undersea dream.

What did it all mean? Glad that was just a dream, I think, looking at the clock. I can get a couple more hours of sleep before the day begins.

Chapter 10

I decide I really need to hit the pause button on any more thoughts about a café/coffee shop for now, anyway. My dream felt too real when Jean walked in and made their comments, even as a jellyfish.

I also decide I need to keep my distance from Ethan for the time being. He is so excited about the coffee shop. Just like in the dream, it feels like he will be pushing me to move forward with the business plans. And I can't focus on too many things at once or I will focus on nothing. Not to mention, I'm hoping to go out with Bryan and I don't want to string Ethan along.

So, I pivot my focus to my real job, at least for today. The deliverables for the website design are still only partly done, and I feel as though I'm scrambling to keep up with the team. Each day I go to work, I try my best to get more mock-ups completed and answer my teammates' questions about the design. But I'm losing track of the overall site and making mistakes.

A button on one page I notice I've named differently on another page...when they're supposed to be the same.

And my day to day is always interrupted by other things.

One day my parents need some help, another day, a cool task force comes along I want to participate in. I know rationally my attention needs to be laser focused on the website design, but my interest sometimes wanes. And the employee resource group on green space redesign sounds so interesting!

I meet with Jean weekly to talk about my performance improvement status. At first, the meetings seem helpful and positive; an opportunity to talk about my priorities and progress. But after a few more meetings, both Jean and I have started to dread them.

"Sophia, the team told me the shopping cart page design is still not done this week. As we discussed last week, that should be your top priority and should have been finished last week. What gives?"

I look away as I'm searching my memory banks for an answer or even a faint recollection of that conversation.

"I thought the Frequently Asked Questions page was the top priority for the week. I've put a lot of my time into that this week. I worked on the shopping cart page but it's true, I didn't finish it."

Jean sighs. "Well, that's unfortunate because we clearly talked about the shopping cart page as a priority last week."

I continue to search my memory banks for what I heard Jean say last week. If I'm being totally honest with myself, I'm drawing a complete blank on this part of the conversation. It's as though someone took an eraser and rubbed out the discussion. The Frequently Asked Questions page has a lot of fun research about the coffee industry in general, and I did enjoy delving into that research. The shopping page is, in comparison, somewhat boring. But I know this explanation is not a good answer to the question Jean asked of "what gives".

"I guess I misunderstood the priorities, Jean. I apologize to you, and I will apologize to the team. I'll get right on that shopping page and finish it up as quickly as possible."

"Please do, Sophia. We hired you to be a part of the team and you're a very important part of the team. If you're falling behind, the whole project is falling behind." Jean looks at Sophia with concern.

"I get that, Jean, really I do. I don't mean to let anyone down and I'm very clear on the priorities now. Thank you for taking the time with me to clear that up. Is there anything else we need to cover today?"

"Unfortunately, Sophia, yes. You have been getting to work late a couple times a week. And when you're behind on deliverables, the optics on that are really bad for the team. I'm not a stickler for when people get to work because everyone has dentist appointments and so on, but it's another area the team is coming to me and raising concerns about."

"But Jordan didn't get in until 10 yesterday and Max strolls in every day at least 20 minutes late," I respond indignantly.

"Sophia, I'm aware of Jordan's and Max's arrival times, and I'm working with them on that. But to be totally honest, because they aren't on performance improvement right now, they're less of a concern. I hope you understand *that's* exactly what I mean when I say it's an optics thing."

I think back to the days I arrived later than I'd planned. Again, every day is different. One day, I can't find my keys. Another day, I have to get gas on the way.

The universe seems to be conspiring against me getting to work on time. Or…or, maybe I need to rethink how much time I need to get ready to be on time. Maybe I should get up earlier and leave some buffer in the schedule for the inevitable bumps along the way.

Jean clears their throat. "Sophia, this is the part where you give me feedback to let me know you are hearing my message."

I realize once again I've gone off into my own thoughts and left an uncomfortable silence in the conversation with Jean.

"Yes, sorry, I hear you and I was thinking of what I could do to course correct, like leaving more time for the unexpected."

"Exactly, Sophia, that's a great thought. Now please go do whatever you need to do to get those deliverables done and be on time. You know these are difficult conversations and the only positive outcome will be if you take what I'm telling you seriously and make some changes."

"Aye aye, captain." I make a weak attempt at humor and head back to my cubicle.

"Have a good day."

"You too. And thank you for working with me on this, Jean.

"I do appreciate your time and how this is an impactful topic for our team. I'll work on getting better."

Chapter 11

Later that day, I decided to go to the bookstore where I saw Bryan in hopes of seeing him again. I wander among the dusty shelves and breathe in the scent of old books. I pretend to look interested in the books Bryan mentioned were of interest to him. The section on sports fiction isn't huge, so I figure I can spot him easily if he does walk in. I pick up a few books and check out the story lines.

Usually, these books are about a player who has challenges of some type that relate to teamwork and overcoming some obstacles. OK, so not too unlike the books I usually read.

I'm getting into a book about a young player who hopes to become a professional football player when I hear my name.

"Sophia, so great to see you!" Bryan is walking down the aisle with a pile of books. He doesn't look at all like a seahorse, I'm immensely relieved and happy to see. In fact, he looks downright handsome dressed in well-fitting jeans and a collared white shirt that highlights his slightly sun browned forearms.

"I was just stocking up on books for a visit to my mom at the hospital."

"Oh, does your mom like sports fiction?"

"No, not at all, these are for me."

"Ahhh, gotcha. This book sounds interesting. Have you read it?" I showed Bryan the book I was looking at when he walked in.

"No, I haven't read that one. The main character doesn't strike my fancy."

I puzzle at that comment because the main character seems like a wonderful person of color with a tough upbringing. He actually seems inspiring to me, but I've only skimmed the book.

I wait a beat to see if Bryan explains himself further but after an awkward moment or two of silence, it appears he's not going to comment any more. I then wonder if I should ask about Bryan's mom. I don't really know what's going on and whether it will upset Bryan to talk about it more. So, I settle on a fairly neutral opening question.

"What's on your agenda today, besides visiting your mom?"

"Well, I hope to get out of there quickly. You know, hospitals depress me. I'm going to go golfing later this afternoon. I'm excited to find there are lots of places to golf around here."

I nod. "Yes, that's one business that we seem to have enough of here. Our weather stays nice even in the colder months, so people who like to golf can get out almost year round. And as with most things, there are the "touristy" places and the places where the locals go."

"Oh, interesting, what's the difference between the two?" Bryan asks.

"Well the touristy places are closer to the beach and the areas with all the condos on the northside of town, where the locals' places are further inland. The locals' places are a bit more of a drive but lots prettier, I think. They have more trees and greenery. Also, as you'd expect, the touristy places get crazy crowded in June through August.

"The locals' places stay relatively quieter even in the summer months.

"Also, the touristy places try to attract business with flashy flags and just feel a bit...ummm...over the top with their landscaping.

"One place even has bushes they trim in the shape of a golf club and a tee. And they're super green all the time even when the weather has been dry. They water the heck out of those places. The locals' places have a more, how shall I say, natural look especially when we don't get a ton of rain. And the touristy places have fancy clubhouses and try to sell lots of drinks."

"I'm always a fan of a good margarita after a round of golf.

"Heck, even before a round of golf." Bryan says. "I think I'll check out the touristy places first. They sound like my style."

"Speaking of margaritas, what places do you recommend for good ones?"

My heart skips a beat, hoping this conversation will lead to a date.

"Yeah, like the golf courses, there are touristy places and local places. Tourists enjoy the Margarita Mayhem spot on the beach. It's a mobile set up; you know, like a food truck but they don't sell food there. They have a bunch of different flavors, and you can get any of the flavors on the rocks or frozen, more like a shake. I'm not a margarita fan but they seem to be popular.

"Locals prefer the margaritas at the Mexican restaurant over on Broad Avenue, behind the downtown area. It's actually pretty close to where I work, and they also do awesome taco specials on Tuesdays. They serve tacos in both the Americanized and authentic Mexican style. The American version has ground beef, flour tortillas, tomatoes, iceberg lettuce, cheddar cheese, refried beans, and sour cream. I prefer the Mexican version which includes marinated meat and veggies, corn tortillas, onions, cilantro, sliced cucumber, chili peppers and radishes."

"Wow, you seem to know a lot about this restaurant and these yummy tacos. You're making me hungry just describing them."

"Yep, we go to lunch there at least a couple times a month. They have a cute patio outside also. You asked about margaritas. I've never tried one there, you know, since I usually go over for lunch, but they pretty much just have the traditional flavor, lime. And you can get them on the rocks or frozen. Friends who have tried them rave about them. I don't know what makes them better, but I have friends who say they are AMAZING."

"Well, Sophia, I would be honored if you would join me one day for tacos and margaritas at that place, maybe one day after work?"

A spike of thrill courses through my body and a wide grin spreads across my face.

"I'd love to, can you do Friday?"

"You bet, would you like to meet there, or do you want me to pick you up?"

"We can meet there. I'll already be right there at my work, and I'll just walk on over."

"Wonderful, see you Friday."

"See you Friday."

Chapter 12

The rest of the week seems to drag by as I wait for my date with Bryan. Work is busy and I continue to find it difficult to set and keep the priorities in focus and moving forward. On Wednesday, the team encountered an urgent issue with one of the websites. A virus had been introduced that made it unstable. I'm on the new development team and I'm not expected to jump into the issue based on my job description. However, it's somehow exciting and fascinating and all anyone seems to be talking about at work. So I have a case of "FOMO", fear of missing out if I don't attend the calls with the vendors and the team to work on resolving the problem. It's a virus that's impacting other companies' websites as well, so it's on the news feeds and front and center in day to day conversations.

I put on headphones to minimize the background noise of the team going about with the fixes and try to get back to my coffee website deliverables. By the end of the week, I need to complete the design of four additional pages and, as Jean reminded me, the top priority shopping cart page *must* be done. I run into a snag while I work on the mocked up page and need a developer to help. But all the developers are tied up with the production issue, so I decide to set that aside for the time being and pivot back to another design. One of the pages is all about fair trade coffee business and how different areas of the world are working on making conditions better for the employees growing the coffee.

This page requires a deep dive into the industry and practices, and I find myself mesmerized by the topic.

First, I learned that coffee is grown in what is known as the "bean belt", an area near the equator that has the right growing conditions for producing coffee beans. Around 50 countries make up the area and around 12 million farms produce coffee. Coffee farmers in only two of the top ten producing countries, Vietnam and Brazil, were making enough money to escape poverty in 2018-2019. Child labor was reported in seventeen of the countries.

The nature of coffee growing cycles also plays a factor in the economic picture. Unusual weather patterns such as frost in South America have recently wreaked havoc with the industry. And like most products, rising production costs after COVID have impacted farmers' ability to make a decent wage in the coffee trade. And most of the profits are made not by the farmers producing the coffee, but by the roasters and retailers who have the most power in pricing and trading terms. The people who are picking the beans are seasonal workers who are paid on a day-to-day basis, usually at less than a living wage. Women are often doing the lower paid work of harvesting and cultivation while men are given higher paid jobs in logistics and pruning.

Even beyond the plight of the workers, production of coffee has other environmental impacts that are concerning. As coffee producers struggle to obtain decent growing locations, deforestation and biodiversity loss is on the rise. Producers often use a method called "wet coffee production" which uses huge amounts of water.

I shake my head and try to avoid delving further into the research. I'm thinking about how to lay all of this out in an infographic page that can hold the interest of a casual coffee website consumer without getting too depressing or dramatic. It's important that people understand the issue at a high level and how by buying coffee labeled as fair trade, they are helping in a small way. But like so many things in life, the picture is complicated.

I decide to lay out the page with big headings that can be clicked to get more information on each topic. Each large topic will have a single sentence that quickly summarizes the challenge then a "+" for a reader to learn more.

I'm starting to mock up the topic of labor issues when Jean stops by my desk. Jean gives a thumbs up, seeing me using headphones to cancel out noise.

I remove the headphones and smile. "What's up, Jean?"

"Glad to see you using the headphones, that's hopefully helping you with noise in this setting?"

"Oh yes, almost too much. I've been really into reading up on the industry." I start telling Jean about all the interesting things I'm learning about fair trade coffee and how I'm planning to lay out the page.

Jean frowns slightly. "Hmmm, that's all fascinating but does that mean you're done with the shopping cart page?"

"Um, no...I need one of the developers for that and they're all caught up in that production issue."

Jean's frown deepens. "Sophia, there are six developers on the team. One of them should be able to help you with this snag. We've talked about this as the highest priority, and we can't slow down. Have you asked one of them to help you and they said no?"

"Well, no, I just assumed none of them could be pulled away from the virus work."

Jean sighs deeply. "Sophia, they need you to finish this up so they can move forward on it. I have no doubt we can pull one of them to help. Do you want me to go with you to get one of them?"

"Yes, that's probably a good idea. That way if they do say no, you can help with the priority call."

Jean and I walk over to where the developers are huddled around a large monitor pointing at code. I explain the snag I've run into with the coffee website shopping cart page and ask if one of them can help.

Christopher says "I can help. Gimme five minutes and I'll come to your cube. We really need this design, and the team here can do without me for the time being, they have it under control. I'll see you soon."

Jean nods and thanks Christopher for stepping away.

"So, Sophia, you have what you need now to keep going on the shopping page. I know you have other deliverables due but until that's done, I want you to move mountains to keep moving forward. Come get me if you need me to help with anything else that gets in your way."

"Got it, Jean. Thank you and I'm on it."

"I hope so, Sophia, I really hope so."

Chapter 13

Friday finally arrives, the day I'm meeting Bryan at the Mexican restaurant after work. I packed a change of clothes and some makeup to freshen up at the end of the day so I can leave straight from work and meet him there.

At around 4:30, I'm ready to head to the restroom to start freshening up and changing clothes when Jean stops at my desk.

"Hey Sophia, how did the rest of the shopping cart page design go after Christopher helped you with the one issue?"

My excitement for my date is suddenly squashed and my stomach clenches. I prepare myself to answer by taking a deep, calming breath.

"Christopher was able to help me with the issue I ran into midweek. But…"

Jean's expression darkens. "But what? I don't like the sound of this."

"But I showed Christopher all the research I had done on the coffee industry and fair trade practices and we both got really jazzed about that subject. We decided to work more on that together. Christopher was showing me some really cool features we can use to expand the relevant text and…"

Jean's cheeks flush. They interrupt and raise their voice.

"Sophia, the shopping cart page is part of the minimum delivery we agreed to, and the coffee industry part is a nice feature to have.

"You and Christopher can't make the call to switch that priority without discussing it with the team. And frankly, I can't see how the priorities would change because the whole reason for the site is to sell coffee which requires a shopping cart feature! Do you understand what I'm saying?"

I bow my head and nod. "Yes, I see what you mean. I'm sorry, Jean. I can work the weekend on the shopping cart page if I need to."

Jean considers this.

"I would rather not have anyone working the weekend. But in this case, it seems like that's the right call. If the shopping cart page design isn't done for the team by Monday, we're all in trouble. And I probably don't have to say this, but this does NOT look good for you on your performance status."

"I get it, Jean. I'll work on it over the weekend and again, I'm sorry."

Jean sighs. "I wish you would have completed it this week so you didn't have to work the weekend, but it looks like our only choice at this point. I hope you have a good weekend anyway."

"You too, Jean, you too," I respond.

My enthusiasm for my date with Bryan is considerably dampened by the prospect of working the weekend. But I resolve to set aside work for the next few hours and enjoy the evening as much as I can. Considering I'll be hunched over a laptop for much of the weekend, I may as well let my hair down for the time being.

I go to the restroom, freshen up my makeup and change clothes. I realize I'm going to be late to meet Bryan because of the conversation I just had with Jean. Ten minutes after I was supposed to meet Bryan, I text an apology and let him know I will be there in ten minutes.

Yikes, twenty minutes late for our first date. That's not a good way to start, I think as I walk to the restaurant.

When I arrive, Bryan already is most of the way through his first margarita. "I hope you don't mind that I got started."

"Oh no, I understand, and I am sooooo sorry to be late."

I describe my conversation with Jean and the reason for my lateness to Bryan.

"That sucks, Sophia, sorry to hear that. But for now, let's get you a drink."

I take a moment to study Bryan's face as he tries to get the waiter's attention.

His face was a study in classical perfection, as though sculpted by a master hand. The planes and angles of his features came together with a flawless symmetry. His jawline was strong and chiseled, a perfect frame for the quiet intensity that lingered in his gaze. Eyes the color of a stormy sea, deep and mesmerizing, held a thousand unspoken stories, their allure only heightened by the soft sweep of dark lashes and the arch of expressive brows.

His cheekbones, high and defined, cast subtle shadows that played across his face, adding a depth and mystery to his expression. His nose, straight and noble, led down to lips that were both full and inviting, with a curve that hinted at secrets only the heart could understand. There was a warmth in his smile, a gentle curve that softened the stark beauty of his face, making it not just handsome but irresistibly captivating. His hair, a tousled crown of rich, deep brown waves, fell effortlessly around his face, each strand catching the light like a cascade of silk.

Even the brown stubble that graced his jaw added to his allure, a roughness that hinted at wildness beneath the refined exterior. His skin, sun-kissed and smooth, glowed with a vitality that spoke of youth and vigor, yet there was a timelessness to his beauty, as if he had stepped out of a legend or a dream.

His good looks probably mean he can have any woman he chooses. That thought puts me in an uneasy state of mind. While I'm considered traditionally attractive, I'm not a knockout. I have chocolate brown hair with lighter eyes, almost the color of whiskey. But I don't have an hourglass figure or a mane of wild blonde hair.

I once again tried to set aside the sense of unease and focus back on having a nice evening with good food and a handsome young man.

My first margarita goes down smoothly, and I order another as Bryan and I get to know each other better.

I learn more about his family, his sports interests and his hobbies. Besides golf, he's an avid birdwatcher. He starts to talk about all the birds he's been seeing here in Virginia that he doesn't see often back at home.

I find myself slightly bored by his talk of sanderlings and two types of pelicans and... did I know how many kinds of gulls they get in Virginia, especially during the migration season? My mind wanders back to the work I have ahead of me on the weekend. Maybe another margarita will help ease my mind from all these unpleasant thoughts of work and my insecurity. And maybe it will even make Bryan's explanation of shorebirds more interesting. I gesture to the waiter for another margarita.

When the waiter delivers the next round, I'm surprised to see him take two glasses away. This is my third margarita. I'd better watch it, I think. But it goes down smoothly as Bryan continues to describe the habitats where the shorebirds like to hang out around Lyndville. How exciting, I think wryly. Maybe this last margarita will make this conversation more interesting...

By the end of the night, I'm fuzzy on how many margaritas I actually drank. Each time my glass was empty, Bryan tried to order another. And the margaritas did make the bird talk more enjoyable. Bryan invited me to go on a birding adventure with him in the future and I agreed. Neither of us were in any shape to drive, so we shared an Uber back. When the Uber arrived at my place, Bryan walked me to my door. In our tipsy states, we shared a sloppy hug and near kiss, both smelling like a margarita factory. Despite his massive good looks, our departing hug and kiss didn't bring on sparks. But I chalked that up to the endless margaritas and a long work week.

Maybe the next time we're together, sparks will start, I think as I close the door and stumble into my apartment.

Chapter 14

Saturday morning, I woke up with a headache and was startled that I had slept past sunrise. I usually woke up well before dawn to start my day. My memories of the prior night came back in chunks. I remembered the difficult conversation with Jean at the end of the day and how it now meant I needed to work this weekend. I recalled the unease I felt at the beginning of my date with Bryan, not because of Bryan, but because of the anxiety my work situation caused. Oh crap, and I was late! Although I had tried, I hadn't been able to set it aside. Which, if I was being honest with myself, was a large part of the reason I drank so much. Bryan had also encouraged me to drink more than I usually did.

I gulped down a large glass of water, took some ibuprofen, and started a pot of coffee.

I started to mentally plan the weekend. I need to do laundry, clean my apartment, and visit my folks. And I need to get the shopping cart page design done.

UGGGGGHH. With the headache that was persisting, I decided to put off the working part of my weekend until later and start with a visit to my folks.

My mom greets me with a warm hug, as usual, and my dad calls from the sunroom, "Hey, Champ, glad to see you!" We catch up on my parents' latest medical appointments, my mom's volunteer work at the humane society, and my work week. I decide not to mention my date with Bryan and my lingering headache...although I'm not sure why. I guess I just don't want to talk about it.

My parents have always been entirely supportive of whomever I date, but for some reason, I'm hesitant to mention Bryan.

"Would you like some tea or coffee, Sophia?

"I want you to meet the latest litter of kittens I'm fostering here. Oh, and I want to show you what I'm doing with my garden."

The kittens are adorable and climb all over each other to get into my and my mom's laps. They are all the colors of the cat rainbow; an orange male, a black female and two male tabbies with brown, black and white stripes.

They chase each other's tails, sneak up on each other to attack, and wrestle for what seems like hours.

My mom shows me around the garden and how she is moving the herbs to a sunnier spot and putting in new shade perennials. "Do you need any help with this, Mom?"

"I'd love some help digging the holes for the new perennials. Oh, and getting that darned lemon balm out. It's almost a weed now the way it spreads. On second thought, I should treat it like a weed and make sure I get the roots out."

My headache has subsided with the ibuprofen, water, and coffee moving through my system. I still feel the effects of the alcohol as if my brain is covered in a light layer of fuzz, but I'm physically feeling ok. So, I spend some time helping my mom with the garden.

Sometime in early afternoon, my mom brings out turkey sandwiches and more iced tea to fortify me.

After we've made good progress on the garden project, I decide I need to catch up with my dad. Although he was in the sunroom the whole time we were gardening, I hadn't really had much conversation with him yet. He updates me on the new book series he's reading and his trip to the library on Tuesday, the new dentist he's seeing next week, and all the things going on in his medical life. His primary care doctor has referred him to a specialist for his digestive issues out of an abundance of caution. He doesn't think there's anything particularly bad going on, but maybe some more adjustments in his meds and his diet will help him feel better.

In the back of my mind, I'm thinking about the chores I still have left to do at my apartment and the looming work deadline.

I decide it's time for me to head out and I'm shocked to see it's nearly 4:00 by the time I bid my parents farewell.

As I drive back to my apartment, I decide to get started on the laundry and cleaning. The clutter of my apartment and the pile of dirty laundry would make it hard to focus anyway. So, I haul out my vacuum, toss in a load of laundry, and start up my favorite cleaning playlist to keep me energized. I hum as I cleans and sometimes sing out loud. Pharrell Williams "Happy" buoys my spirits as I dust. I belt it out, singing into my vacuum cleaner as a microphone.

"Clap along if you feel like a room without a roof. Because I'm happy..clap along if you feel like happiness is the truth. Because I'm happy...clap along if you know what happiness means to you..."

At that phrase, I stop and take a breath. Those lyrics hit me now for some reason. Do I know what happiness means to me? What a great question, Pharrell.

The sun is drifting below the horizon as I fold the last basket of laundry. I decide the work on the shopping cart page will need to wait until Sunday. I've had a long, busy, and productive day and I have no energy left today.

I know in my heart the work will always be there, but my parents won't so I'm glad I spent much of the day with them.

Chapter 15

Sunday morning, I slept past my normal workday wakeup. I stretch luxuriously on the soft flannel sheets and enjoy the feeling of not having to jump out of bed and head straight to work. Knowing, however, that I do have to work today comes crashing back and limits my enjoyment of the morning for a few minutes. My mind goes to how I'm going to handle the sales and promotional aspect of the coffee website and whether I'll put coupons on the page or separate that out completely and…I stop myself on that thought train. For now, I decide to set that aside, enjoy a leisurely cup of coffee and a slower start to the morning as usual.

Bryan didn't text me on Saturday but mid-morning, my phone sends the happy chime of a text from him. He apologizes for not reaching out on Saturday and explains he spent the day at the hospital with his mom and dad. His mom had a brief setback and was doing better by the end of the day, but he was preoccupied for most of the day.

I text back that it's no problem and I totally understand. I was caught up with my own parents most of the day on Saturday also, and so I definitely got it. Bryan asks me if I'd like to go out to lunch today or one day this week.

I want to say yes but my work situation needs to be addressed. I ponder if I can go out to lunch with Bryan and get the shopping cart page design done. I think so…if our lunch is over by 2, I'll still have the rest of the day to work on it.

"I'd be delighted to have lunch with you. Where do you want to go?"

My mind drifts back to thoughts of his stormy colored eyes, his thick lashes and strong jaw. I feel a thrill of excitement and anticipation to watch his handsome face throughout a meal without the dulling sense I had on Friday from the margaritas.

"You know I'm new here, so I don't know much about the restaurant scene. What do you like? What do you suggest?"

"The diner over by the beach actually serves a pretty good brunch. Their coffee isn't the best, but their omelets are amazing. They do just about any combination of meats and veggies you can think of. And they have four different types of cheese, including a smoked gouda that makes the omelet flavor just over the top delicious."

"Sounds great, Sophia, may I pick you up or do you want to meet there?"

"I'll take a ride. That sounds great. What time?"

"I'll be there at 11:45, how about?"

"Fantastic, see you then."

I finish my regular Sunday household chores after that, feeling good about having clean laundry, a full refrigerator, and clean floors. My mind is much more peaceful when my surroundings are clean and in order.

Bryan shows up right on time and we head out to the diner. When we arrive, the line is out the door. We take a pager device and agree to walk on the beach while we wait.

While we walk, I learn more about Bryan's mom's illness. The doctors haven't yet figured out what's going on, but she has attacks of breathing difficulty. They've ruled out some of the most serious illnesses, which is a relief. Her lungs show no signs of cancer or other lesions.

They're hoping the ocean air might help some with the condition. She is going to have an extensive set of allergy testing soon. In the meantime, she needs to have assistance breathing from time to time, hence the hospital visits.

As we walk, Bryan points out some of the shorebirds he's been telling me about. He points out a cute little bird running across the beach and tells me it's a Solitary Sandpiper. He points out a gull and tells me it's a Lesser Black-backed Gull.

"Oh, and there's a Pectoral Sandpiper!"

"Is that one that works out a lot?" I joke, "Get it, pectoral like in muscles?"

Bryan frowns for a moment and then gets the joke and smirks.

"How in the world do you tell these apart?" I wonder. "All I can see is there are some gulls and some little birds that do more walking on the shore than flying."

"Practice is all. I learned the big things that set them apart first and then learned more details as I got into birding. I could talk all day long about the interesting habits of these guys and their migration patterns and–"

Just then the pager that tells us our table is ready sounds. We head back towards the restaurant and a waiter leads us to a private table at the back of the patio. We can still hear the waves and calls of the birds as we sit down and begin to peruse the menu.

"Yes, stop me if you get tired of hearing me go on and on about the birds. I can get carried away, especially when I'm in a new place and I'm seeing things I've not seen before or haven't seen for a while."

"Oh, it's interesting all right and maybe someday I'll go birdwatching with you. But for now, I'm going to figure out my order, I'm starving. What time is it anyway?"

"It's a little after one. I guess it took longer than they thought for a table to open up. I hope that's not a problem."

I inwardly groan...the weekend is slipping away, and I haven't done a thing to finish up my work that needs to be done by Monday. I paste a smile on my face and say, "Oh nothing pressing that I can't finish up before the end of the day."

By the time Bryan and I order, get our food and eat, it's nearly 3:00. The meal was delicious, and I enjoyed spending more time with Bryan. But I know I need to get home and crack open my laptop. I know I probably seemed antsy as the afternoon went on, and I wish I had told him the whole story about what I needed to finish. But I didn't want to weigh down the mood with work woes, so I kept it all inside.

Once I get home, I skip dinner and work on the shopping cart page for the next several hours. I'm mentally and physically exhausted by 9:00 and feel like I've made enough progress to call it a day. I fall into bed and sleep fitfully…again, this time with coffee baskets and online shopping dreams keeping me from deep, restful sleep.

Chapter 16

The next morning, I feel more than a little cranky from the poor night of sleep I had. Add to that, I'm staring at a full week of work ahead. And I feel a creeping sense of dread to face Jean and the team after having let them down last week on the project. I remember the Garfield cartoons my parents have in one of their stashes of boxes where Garfield hates Mondays. I momentarily wonder why he hates Mondays since, presumably, as a cat, he doesn't have to go to work. I suppose it's the sense of repetition in his life and the reminder of the passage of time.

I shake myself out of this reverie and head into work.

At the team standup meeting, I walk them through my completed work on the shopping cart page design.

They have lots of questions, but in general, seem satisfied they can move forward from here on the development.

Jean is less than enthusiastic, but nods in my direction at the end of the meeting with a look that says I dodged a bullet by pulling through.

Ethan looks especially happy and maybe a little proud? of my progress.

I feel as though a weight has been lifted from my shoulders…at least for today.

After the team meeting, Ethan asks me if I'd like to join him for lunch or a walk today. I think briefly of my date with Bryan and whether this would make him angry or jealous. I conclude no; that Bryan would understand going somewhere with Ethan would just be a couple of co-workers shooting the breeze about work. I agree to head out to lunch with Ethan, telling myself it's not-a-date-but-a-lunch-with-a-coworker get together.

Throughout the rest of the morning, the team peppers me with follow up questions about the shopping cart page design. I get so many instant message chats and texts, I can barely keep up. The team has found a couple of flaws in how the webpages flow and they're all asking questions at the same time. I feel overwhelmed and out of sorts by the time noon rolls around. I could keep working through lunch and ask Ethan for a rain check, but I think stepping away will help me clear my mind.

When Ethan stops by my cubicle at noon, I feel relieved and…something else I'm not sure how to name.

I notice more about Ethan in that moment than I had before. How he has a dimple on his right cheek when he smiles. How his greenish gray eyes are almond shaped and expressive, conveying warmth and friendliness.

Ethan's build is athletic but not overly muscular, and he gives off a vibe of being healthy but not overly concerned with appearances. Today, he's dressed in well-fitting jeans, a plain gray t-shirt, a plaid button down, and comfortable Converse sneakers. He looks confident, approachable, and down to earth. There's an easy-going charm about him that makes him completely relatable.

But most of all, I know I'm going to be heard and understood by Ethan on our not-date and that feels amazing.

I once again briefly consider if this is fair to Bryan and if this is fair to Ethan. I conclude that yes, this is a good idea, and yes, I may have different feelings for Ethan than I realized, but for now, I'm going to just roll with it.

As we walk to lunch, Ethan and I discuss our respective weekends. Ethan volunteers at the same shelter as my mom, and he tells me about a litter of kittens that came in over the weekend that someone had found under their porch. The momma was feral and the kittens were frightened of humans but clearly needed help.

I describe my weekend too, but I gloss over the date with Bryan and the too many margaritas part. I talk about how I kept meaning to get my work done but kept putting it off.

Ethan nods knowingly and says "Yep, totally get it. I have the same problem at times with getting started on something that I know will suck. Also, I tend to underestimate how long things will take. Or when I'm thinking through what I need to get done, I forget a big chunk of it and then whatever it is will take me twice as long as I had originally planned. That's my ADHD talking, for me, anyway."

"What do you do to manage that, Ethan? You always seem to get things done and don't have the team mad at you all the time like I do."

"It's one of the things I've been working on with my therapist. Knowing I have this tendency for my brain to crap out on me at times, I have to be pretty structured with planning my days. It's taken me a while to…and I use air quotes here… 'perfect' my planning system, but I finally have a pretty good handle on how to do it. I have a template I can share if you'd like. I number everything on my to do list so I know what needs to get done early in the day and if something needs to get done before something else.

"I also find a quote of the day to put me in the right frame of mind.

"Sometimes I need to practice acceptance, sometimes I need to remind myself how grateful I am for being alive. Reading through quotes and finding the perfect one helps me start my day on the right footing. And it helps me explore my feelings sometimes to find words that resonate. Hope that doesn't sound too woo-woo.

"And…I know it sounds a little complicated, but it has made a huge difference in my life as far as accomplishing what I want to accomplish."

I puff out a deep breath. "Yes, that sounds really hard, but it also sounds like something I should try. If it works for you, maybe it will work for me too. I really don't want to lose my job. I think Jean is at wits end with the issues I've been having. Please do share your template, and maybe we can have another conversation later in the week after I check out the template, digest it, and hear more?"

I also want to spend more time with Ethan to get that same sense of feeling completely heard and understood. And his boyish good looks and charm don't hurt.

"I'd be happy to, I'll send that to you today and maybe we can have lunch again on Wednesday?"

"Great, thank you so much. I appreciate your listening and helping so much, more than I can express," I reply.

"No problem, Sophia. Let's get back to the office and I'll send that to you right away."

Ethan winks and my heart skips a beat. He looks so cute and...that dimple...and I remind myself Ethan is just a friend.

"THANK YOU, Ethan, my friend...so much."

Chapter 17

My best friend, Amira, is due back from her backpack trek across France on Tuesday.

I can't wait to hear all about her adventures and catch up. Having her gone has been a missing piece of my life. I'm proud of Amira for having taken such a cool trip by herself…going to a foreign land, staying in hostels, and being out alone for nearly two months. We're planning to get together Thursday before work, since Amira will still be adjusting to the east coast time and recovering from her jet lag. Since France is six hours ahead, Amira will be wide awake in the morning and ready to get breakfast at the diner.

When Thursday rolls around, I hop out of bed with excitement building to hear about Amira's trip. And I can't wait to tell Amira all about my date with Bryan, my difficulties at work, and my conflicted feelings about Ethan. Amira is right on time and looks rested, fit, and serene. Her caramel skin is glowing and her mahogany eyes twinkle.

"Oh my gosh, France must suit you, you look tres belle.

"You look so toned and so calm."

Amira laughs. "Well, my trek was nearly across the width of the country and that meant I had to walk around ten miles a day. So, yeah, that will tend to get a person into pretty good shape. I was also carrying my backpack with my clothes and all so that added to the challenge for my body. And walking just really helps me clear my head, so that's probably the calm. I had multiple hours to think and meditate. It was better than any therapy for me…think a little, set stuff aside, think a little more. I need quiet time and being away from people sometimes to get centered."

"Wow, that sounds amazing. I'm so happy it was such a great experience. You're so strong. Your parents named you well.

"Show me pictures! Tell me about all the places you stayed, all the people you met. I'm sure you met some characters along the way."

Amira pulls out her phone and starts to scroll through the photos, telling me about each of her stops, the people she occasionally walked with, and the food. The food sounds like it was one of the best parts of the trip. How Amira could eat a pain au chocolat, essentially a croissant filled with a chocolate paste every day and look more fit on the other side is a miracle to me. And she describes all the delicious cheeses and wines she tried along the way and how much she will miss all of that being back in the United States.

"But enough about my trip, catch me up on everything I've missed in your life these last two months."

I blew out a breath…where to even begin.

I start by telling Amira all about my dad's medical situation. Amira and I have been friends since middle school and Amira knows my parents very well.

"So all in all, Dad is doing well for his age. The surgery went well, and the lump was benign."

"Oh, thank goodness. That must have been a hard journey for all of you worrying about what that was," Amira replies.

"Yep, it was difficult. It was one of the things that also impacted my work. You'll never believe this but I'm on a 'performance plan' at work. I'm skating on thin ice, I guess. because I was having such a hard time getting my work done.

"I say was past tense but I still am. I just had another round of that last week where I was supposed to complete a design for a shopping cart page, and I worked on another page altogether.

"Plus, I was helping my parents with the paperwork and the day of the surgery and so on. You know how hard it is to focus at work to begin with, let alone having all these distractions."

"Woof, Sophia, so where do you stand with all of that now?"

"I'm not sure, honestly. I meet with Jean every week and we talk through it. Jean is very levelheaded and supportive, but this last situation was not a good reflection on me. I guess I'll find out more when we meet."

I'm saving the best part of my story for last.

"And…there's another set of distractions that I can't wait to tell you about." I grin widely, make a dreamy face and put a palm over my heart.

"Spill, Sophia, don't keep me in suspense! You're such a drama queen."

"I've met a new guy. Bryan is his name, he's new in town and he's movie star handsome.

"I'm talking the whole package…eyes the color of the sea, dark lashes and perfectly shaped brows, a chiseled jawline and a mouth I just want to devour."

Amira squeals in delight and happiness for me.

"So you've gone on a date? Multiple dates? You've ridden his high horse? You've moved in together?"

I chuckle.

"Definitely not the high horse yet. We've just gone on a couple of dates. Well, I'm not sure if you can count the first time we met at the bookstore as a date. I stalked him there and so maybe that wouldn't count as a date."

"Wow, I'm so happy for you. But what about Ethan? I always thought the two of you had good chemistry and he's such a…I don't know, he's so down to earth and charming."

"Well, Amira, I'm trying to figure that out myself. I have spent a lot of time with Ethan in the last few weeks and you're right…we have some chemistry. I've noticed he's also pretty cute. He's been so helpful with all the crap going on at work, a shoulder to lean on so to speak.

"And did you know he has ADHD? I'm sure he wouldn't mind me telling you all of this. He talks about it openly and honestly, including about how he's managing it. It's so refreshing to hear him talk so...I don't know...hopefully, I guess, about a difficulty that could really slow him down. But he's managing to survive it and...really thrive. He's living like that Maya Angelou quote."

I look it up and read it to Amira.

"My mission in life is not merely to survive but to thrive; and to do so with some passion, some compassion, some humor and some style."

I ponder all of this for a minute. "I hadn't really thought about Ethan as anything more than a friend, but somehow that feels like it's changing. I have such a comfortable connection and so much respect for him."

Amira grins broadly and says in a sing-song voice "Sophia has a crush on two boys. How fun! The plot thickens."

Chapter 18

Amira and I part ways around 8:30. I head in to work while Amira heads home to continue unpacking and doing laundry. I find myself more than a little jealous that Amira doesn't have to go into a boring, sterile office building and sit in a cubicle all day. While I generally enjoy my work and I'm fascinated by the coffee industry topic now, I feel the mundane nature of the work and the repetition today in particular. I'm feeling my inner Garfield today.

When I think about Amira in France, taking a risk on what she'll do for employment when she gets back, taking a risk going to a new part of the world, I feel a bit…what is it? Confined, too risk-averse in my current situation. But that can't really change anytime soon with my financial situation. I have to keep this job for now so I may as well suck it up, buttercup. Then I think…at least I'll get to see Ethan. Hmm, there it is again, a feeling of wanting to see him even though I keep telling myself Ethan is just a friend. Maybe if I repeat it enough times…it will be true?

Ethan pops his head over my cubicle wall around 10:30 and says, "How's it going, wanna go for a walk? I need to take a break from this mind-numbing spreadsheet I'm working on. My brain is mush."

"Sure, let's go. Give me a minute to check on this message from Christopher."

Christopher is asking me about the design of the pricing functionality. They need to be able to set slightly different prices for the coffee depending on the area of the buyer, but not let that be easily seen by the public. For example, a pound of coffee in New York will cost more than a pound of coffee in Ohio.

I message back, "I missed that in my specs. Can I get back to you later this afternoon?"

Christopher sends an emoji of a person pulling their hair out but responds…"Ah, ok."

I feel that sense of dread again as I'm locking my computer to go for the walk with Ethan. I sort of recall that was outlined in the high level needs for the site, but I hadn't figured out how to represent it in the design I provided to the developers. And from Christopher's reaction, I have a feeling Jean is going to be hearing about it. I briefly wonder if I should skip the walk and get right on making the design updates, but I recall Ethan's tone of voice and decide I need to be there for him like he has been for me. And I remember his dimple and the way his eyes sometimes look green and sometimes more stormy gray and that settles it. I'll go for a quick walk with Ethan, listen supportively, and then jump right back into the website design afterwards.

As Ethan and I walk toward the beach, I feel the muscles relax in my shoulders and neck. I was holding tension there and didn't even realize it. The sound of the waves, the call of the gulls, and the salty tang to the air always set me right. Ethan starts to relax too and describes the ginormous spreadsheet he's working on and the issues he's having with the calculations. I've never been much of a finance or spreadsheet person so I can't offer much other than a supportive "mm hmm" here and an "oh that sucks" there. But it seems to help Ethan to just talk and get out of the office for a brief period. As we walk, he seems to have talked himself into how he's going to troubleshoot and proceed.

I'm pleased this jaunt seems to have helped Ethan get back on track.

"Do you know why a walk like this helps clear your brain?" I ask.

Ethan smiles. "Do tell, oh wise one."

"Well, it increases blood flow, which supplies the oxygen our brains need to function well. Walking releases endorphins, the "feel good" hormones that can reduce stress and anxiety.

"It also has been shown to enhance divergent thinking, the type of thinking that fuels creativity and generates innovative ideas."

"Super cool, Sophia. I knew it was helpful, but I didn't know all of the reasons why."

"Yep, and best of all for you, Ethan, walking has been shown to boost brain connectivity and strengthen neural pathways.

Isn't that one of the main things you mentioned about the challenges of having ADHD?"

"Wow, yes, that's right. And here I thought it was just your amazing listening skills and supportive nodding."

I punch him in the arm. As I do, I notice the rock hard muscle I encounter.

"OK Mr. Smartypants, are you ready to head back into the office?"

"Yes, let's go."

When we arrive back at the building, Christopher is waiting for me at my cube.

"Can we work on this pricing design now? The team really needs to have this figured out in order for it not to block the progress."

"Sure, sorry I was just trying to help Ethan with a problem he's having."

Christopher nods but looks more than a little annoyed, as if Ethan's problem is the last thing he cares about.

"I'll catch you later Sophia. Good luck with this and let me know if I can lend an ear or go on a magical walk with you to help unleash your creativity later."

"You got it, Ethan, take care."

I invite Christopher into my cube and prepare for a long and challenging afternoon of figuring this issue out.

He continues to act annoyed, which doesn't help my overall mood.

We decide to work through lunch and by 5:00 have the problem figured out to where the team can at least proceed.

I'm feeling tired but pleased with the progress. And I think Jean will agree when we meet next. I plan to let Jean know how I also helped Ethan with the problem he was having on his spreadsheet. It can't hurt to throw that in for good measure, right?

Chapter 19

Bryan calls me that evening and asks me out on another date. He suggests we go 'clubbing' and asks me if I like to dance. I giggle at the term 'clubbing' as it relates to Lyndville.

"Well, we don't exactly have a clubbing scene here in Lyndville. This is more of a family vacation destination than a party place."

Bryan sounds a bit deflated and says, "Oh, ok, well what's the closest thing to that then?"

"There's a great small plates restaurant on the beach that has live music on the weekends. People sometimes get up and dance, usually if they are drunk enough."

"Well, would you like to head there? What's it called?"

"Moma's Tapas Bar. I think you'll like it. I'll check what bands are going to be there. My friend Amira worked there before she left for France. She may be working there again, and you can meet her."

"Sounds great, Friday or Saturday night?"

"Let me check out the bands and I'll let you know? Since you want to dance, I'll decide based on the kind of music they play."

"Sounds great, just text me and let me know what night. I'm looking forward to seeing you again."

"Me too." I feel a tingle and warmth spread through my body at the thought of seeing Bryan again. His handsome features come to mind, and I find myself daydreaming about his mouth with his full lips and cupid bow on his upper lip. I wonder if he gets a 5:00 shadow.

"Ahh, Sophia, you still there?"

I startle and realize I've left the conversation hanging.

"Sorry, yes. I was just thinking about the bands I've seen there before," I fib.

"I like all kinds of music so don't worry about that. And like you said, if I'm drunk enough, I'll dance to about any kind of music."

"Sounds good, I'll pick the night and let you know. See you this weekend."

"Yes, see you soon."

★★★

The week goes by at a slower pace than usual, probably because I'm looking forward to my date with Bryan. I decided on Saturday because the band is more upbeat and danceable.

My meeting with Jean to discuss my performance status goes way worse than I expected.

When I explain how I helped Ethan with his spreadsheet, Jean is less than enthusiastic.

"Sophia, I appreciate that you act as a supportive friend, but helping Ethan is not your priority.

"You were slowing down your actual team, you know, the project team working on the coffee website. And the fact that you missed the pricing requirement in your designs was a problem for them. Not to mention the fact that it reflects poorly on your performance. I have no choice but to put you on the last stage of the performance plan. That means if you have any more similar issues in the next month, I'll have to let you go."

I'm stunned and for a few minutes just stare open-mouthed at Jean. I feel tears threatening and swallow because my mouth has gone completely dry.

I take a few deep breaths and say, "Wow, I didn't expect this to be such a big issue. I will do everything I can to keep the team moving forward."

"Please do, Sophia. I'm sorry to have to be the one to deliver this message. For what it's worth, I don't like this part of my job. I think you're extremely talented and smart.

"But you need to not let anything distract you. You seem to get off track with other things, and that's a problem for your teammates. If there is anything I can do to help, let me know."

I'm still in shock but attempt to muster a smile.

"If I think of anything, I'll let you know. Thank you, Jean."

I don't remember leaving Jean's office and stumbling back to my cube. A little while later, Ethan pops into my office.

"You don't look so good, Sophia. Are you ill?"

"I kinda wish I were ill, but no. I just got back from my performance discussion with Jean and they told me basically if I have any more problems, they're going to have to fire me."

"Oh, Sophia. That sooooo sucks, I am so sorry to hear that. Do you want to go for a walk and talk? Do you want a hug?"

"I don't think I should be leaving my cubicle too much based on that conversation. I will take a hug though."

I stand up and wrap my arms around Ethan. The tears that have been threatening finally start to flow. I sob quietly for several minutes and Ethan just hugs me tightly, murmuring "It'll be ok, Sophia…don't worry, Sophia. I know it will be ok."

Despite my fragile state, I can't help but notice how muscular Ethan's back feels.

And how good he smells. I can't quite place the smell but it's some combination of fresh laundry and warm spices. After several minutes, I feel a little better and let go of Ethan. I know I must look like a wreck with puffy, red eyes and tears probably smearing my makeup.

Ethan's look conveys compassion and he seems unbothered by my post-crying puffiness.

"Sorry about that, I think I got your shirt wet with my blubbering. I feel better now."

"I'm glad you feel better and I could care less about my shirt. You know a good cry releases cortisol, the stress hormone so you can soak ten shirts of mine if you need to."

"Thanks, Ethan. I think I'm cried out for now. I guess cortisoled out maybe. I should get back to work."

"I understand. Just let me know though if you need another hug or anything else later today."

"And I'm so sorry my stupid spreadsheet issue became your problem."

"Don't apologize, Ethan. Like Jean says, I get distracted sometimes, and even though I knew what my priorities should have been, I let myself get sidetracked. I could have said no or maybe later, but I didn't. So that's on me."

"Would it help if I talk to Jean?" Ethan asks hopefully.

"No, I don't think it would make any difference. They're probably already writing up whatever official notice and sending it to me and Human Resources already."

"Well, Sophia, I meant it when I said I know it will be ok. I hope this doesn't sound harsh but if you lose this job, it was meant to be. As my wise grandmother once said to me, "If it was meant to be, it will work out and if it wasn't it won't.""

"Wise words, Ethan and Ethan's grandma. Thank you."

Chapter 20

Despite the difficult conversation with Jean, the rest of my week goes pretty well. My mood is elevated by the excitement about a date with Bryan this weekend. And my prediction about a formal write-up from Jean and HR was incorrect, at least for now. The team is making good progress with the designs I delivered, and no major obstacles crop up.

I had decided the best band at Moma's this weekend would be on Saturday. A rock band that plays a mix of their own music and classic rock and roll will be going on stage at 7PM.

We can have a nice tapas meal, a few drinks and some dancing. I know the band also does a few slower songs that will encourage a slow dance with Bryan. I find myself daydreaming about being pressed up against him and looking into his stormy blue gray eyes for a song or two. I have to shake myself back to the present on more than one occasion.

Amira comes over on Saturday for lunch and to help me get ready for my date. I feel like a high schooler with my giddiness and because I'm asking for Amira's help with picking an outfit and doing my makeup.

But it feels sooooo good to have Amira back and I can't wait to do more catching up while we primp.

Amira and I pick out a form fitting gray skirt that hugs my curves and shows a bit of my toned legs…but not too much. We pair it with a white peasant style blouse that is on the sheer side, also showing off my toned arms. I'm going for low key sexy. A chunky silver, gold, and white necklace tops off the outfit and draws the eyes to the smooth skin of my chest. Amira and I agree it will be a nice change since my usual day to day fashion is way less showy and business casual. I tend to wear cargo pants or khakis during the week with a collared shirt…essentially looking like everyone else at work and purposely not showing much of my bodily assets. Although I'm not a fitness nut, I do work in some weight training each week to keep myself in decent shape.

I also decide to do Saturday night makeup and hair. I normally let my hair do its wavy thing with a simple wash and minimal styling during the week. But Saturday, Amira helps me painstakingly blow-dry it straight and flat iron the hell out of it. It's a lot of work, but I feel confident with the sleek, smooth appearance it creates. For my makeup, Amira does a smoky eye look, using deep shades of charcoal, and a rich, walnut brown.

She blends the colors well to create depth and intensity and adds a touch of shimmer on the lids and inner corners for a glamorous effect. Amira chooses a rose tone that compliments my skin tone and blends seamlessly.

For added allure, Amira uses a lip liner to define my lips, creating a fuller appearance and finishes with a satin gloss to make my lips look plump and inviting.

"Hubba hubba" Amira jokes, stepping away from me when my makeup is done.

"What does that even mean, Amira?"

"It means you look hot! I think it's an old timey saying that I heard from my grandparents. But seriously Sophia, You. Look. A-MA-ZING."

Two hours later, when Bryan comes to pick me up, he doesn't say "hubba hubba", but he definitely lights up when he sees my Saturday night date look.

"You look really great, Sophia, just beautiful."

"Thank you," I say, though I can feel the blush rise in my cheeks.

Bryan is dressed in a smart blue Oxford collar shirt that makes his eyes look more blue than gray. His chocolate brown hair looks to be styled and perfectly in place. Is that gel? I think.

"You look great too, Bryan. Ready to go?"

"Yes, let's rock and roll."

At the restaurant, we decide to share several small plates featured on the happy hour menu.

"I love to experience a wide variety of dishes and tastes and this tapas style is the perfect way to do that."

Together we enjoy a steakhouse wedge salad with bacon, candied pecans and dried cranberries, crunchy mac and cheese balls, tiny burger sliders, and salmon bites with a ginger apricot dip.

"MMMMMMmmmm, that was so yummalicious, I'm stuffed."

"Well I hope you can still dance later. How about another drink?" I've already had two glasses of wine and I'm feeling relaxed but not tipsy.

"No, thanks. Last time we went out, I went way too hard on the margaritas and I paid for it the next day. I need to get things done tomorrow, not just wallow around in a hungover stupor."

"No problem. Do you mind if I order another?"

"Of course not, go right ahead."

The band starts playing a little while after we've finished dinner and we enjoy the music for a while. The band is loud so we don't have much more conversation once they start playing. Bryan orders three more drinks and seems to be having a fine time. I surreptitiously sneak glances at Bryan's handsome face when I have a chance. His chiseled jawline, his full lips, and his dark lashes give me a tingle when I think about kissing them. Eventually, the band slows the tempo down and plays an Eric Clapton classic "Wonderful Tonight."

Bryan extends his hand to me and says "Would you care to dance, lovely lady? You do look wonderful tonight."

My heart jumps as we settle into each other's arms on the dance floor. Bryan's hands are low on my waist and I can feel the heat of the connection where his skin touches my back. I wrap my arms around his neck and press the length of my body lightly but snugly to his. Our bodies sway in slow motion, and I find myself wishing the song wouldn't end.

But soon the song does end and I'm getting tired.

I'm used to an early bed time and early wake up time during the week, and it's after ten.

"I don't want to be a party pooper, but would you mind if we leave now? I'm pretty tired."

"No problem. I'll get an Uber. I don't think I should be driving tonight."

"Sounds good."

Once we arrive at my apartment, Bryan asks the Uber driver to wait and walks me to my door. As we stand close, our breaths mingling, time seems to slow.

His eyes lock onto mine, searching for any sign of hesitation. I respond with a soft, almost imperceptible nod, my lips parting slightly in anticipation.

Slowly, he leans in, his hand gently cupping my face, his thumb brushing against my cheek. The warmth of his touch sends a shiver down my spine. Our lips meet in a tender, exploratory kiss, tentative at first, as if savoring the moment we had both longed for.

The kiss deepens, becoming more urgent, as if we were pouring all our unspoken feelings into that single act. My hands find their way to his chest, gripping the fabric of his shirt as if to pull him closer. He responds by wrapping his arm around my waist, drawing me into him until there is no space left between us.

Our lips move in sync, soft yet demanding, each kiss more passionate than the last. The world around us fades away, leaving only the sensation of each other's touch. When we finally pull apart, the lingering taste of the kiss remains on my lips.

"You shouldn't keep your poor Uber driver waiting, he'll give you a bad rating," I joke. "I had a nice time tonight."

"I did too, Sophia, I did too. We should do it again sometime. Have a nice night."

"Have a wonderful night."

Chapter 21

I replay the kiss with Bryan most of the day on Sunday. I go to my folks house for Sunday brunch, to catch up on their week and vice versa.

Mom is a bit distracted when I get there, trying to find the serving spoon for the green beans as I tell her about the date with Bryan.

"Mom, he is so handsome. He looks like he could be on the cover of a men's fashion magazine."

"That's great, honey, where did you go?"

I tell her all about the delicious tapas meal, the band and an abbreviated version of our slow dance and good night kiss.

"Wow, sounds like a wonderful date. Hold on just a minute…" she calls out to my dad in the sunroom, "Frank, have you seen the slotted spoon in your travels around the house?"

"Hmmm, I know we used it on Wednesday and it would have gotten washed and…did you check the junk drawer?"

My mom raises her eyebrow. "No, Frank, why would I check the junk drawer?"

"Well, when I was helping with cleanup that day I was also looking for a screwdriver to fix my sunglasses ,so maybe check there?"

Sure enough when my mom opens the junk drawer, the slotted spoon is there. She chuckles and says under her breath but loud enough for me to hear "That man, I swear he'd lose his head if it wasn't attached to his shoulders."

My parents ask me how things are going at work.

I frown and think about how much I want to tell them about the conversation with Jean. I don't want them to worry, but I want to be honest.

"Work is going so-so. I've had some issues lately, according to my boss Jean anyway, that I need to work on. So that's what I'm doing. I'm trying to take the feedback to heart and make changes. But it's hard. It's not like I'm not trying my best, so it's frustrating to hear this not so great feedback."

My parents nod with compassion and wait for me to continue.

"I don't really want to talk about it anym-"

My dad chimes in, "Remember when I was telling you about my really difficult boss way back when? He told me I was letting my fellow workers down because my numbers were dragging down the rest of the team."

"Jean gave me similar feedback. And I was saying I don't want to talk about it much more, it bums me out. But I also didn't want to keep you in the dark."

"Well, Sophia, we appreciate you telling us about it. And I can also say I'm sure you'll land on your feet no matter what. Things work out for a reason."

"My friend Ethan said the same thing…something his grandmother told him. If it's right, it will work out and if it's not it won't."

"Indeed," my mom says. "This Ethan guy sounds like a good friend and sounding board."

"He really is, Mom. He's been such an amazing listener and supporter at work. He's attractive in a Ryan Gosling kind of way. I don't remember if I told you but he has ADHD. It seems like some of what I'm going through has parallels to his challenges and experiences with ADHD as far as getting distracted and having a hard time foc-"

"Déjà vu!" my dad interrupts. "I feel like I've heard this story before with my old boss! I didn't have a friend like Ethan, though, who had ADHD. I don't think our generation even knew about ADHD. It's more of a recent thing, isn't it?"

"Well, Dad, it's not like ADHD wasn't a thing before. It's more when and how the medical community recognized it and started treating it. In general, we know a lot more about mental health and talk about it more openly now. And I think ADHD was only considered an issue in children. The thought was that kids would outgrow it, which a lot of people do. But for many people, it persists into adulthood, especially if they aren't diagnosed and start treatment."

"Interesting. How common is it, did Ethan mention?" my mom asks.

"I don't think Ethan told me but I did some googling on my own, just for kicks. ADHD is diagnosed in something like 9% of children in the United States which is over 5 million kiddos. I bet if you asked the population of teachers, they would tell you that number is low. Maybe it's contagious."

"Why do you say that, Sophia?"

"Well because teachers probably are the first people who really see it in kids and are the ones who have to deal with the disruptions a kid or kids with ADHD can cause in their classrooms. Especially the hyperactive type.

"Another site I found says ADHD is diagnosed at around 17% for male children and 8% in females. So, almost 2 out of 10 boys and 1 out of 10 girls will have it. And of course, kids imitate one another so if one kid is acting out, other kids in the group will often do the same."

"And what do you mean about the hyperactive type?"

"The hyperactive type is the poster child for ADHD; in other words it's the one that was originally the focus of the diagnosis and treatment.

"Probably because kids, especially boys with ADHD, can cause so much trouble, parents and teachers can't help but notice it more."

I explain the difference between the inattentive and hyperactive types of ADHD, how the hyperactive type is much more noticeable in terms of symptoms such as interrupting.

"Also, some of what I googled shows there's debate about why diagnoses of ADHD are on the rise. Is it mostly social media and familiar characters with ADHD? Is it because young people want the stimulant medications that are used to treat it or the test accommodations? Or, is it that ADHD has truly been underdiagnosed for many years and we're now just figuring that out?"

My mom looks thoughtful. "Like many things, the truth is probably somewhere in the middle."

Resources

How Common Is ADHD

https://www.cdc.gov/adhd/data/index.html

Increasing Awareness of ADHD

https://news.syr.edu/blog/2024/10/04/whats-driving-the-rise-in-adhd-diagnosis-among-children-and-adults/

Chapter 22

Monday dawns a beautiful day in Lyndville, as it usually is in the fall. The temperatures have dropped some, at least overnight to perfect sleeping weather. The days are low humidity but get warm enough to take off sweaters and jackets and enjoy some Vitamin D. I wake up super early with worries of how my work week will go.

And what my feelings for Bryan and Ethan mean. I decide to walk to work today to allow my mind to take in and appreciate my lovely home town.

Lyndville offers a perfect blend of historic charm and coastal beauty. Its wide, sandy beaches are serene and less crowded than those of larger resort towns, making it an ideal spot for relaxation.

My hometown is known for its preserved Victorian homes, charming bed and breakfasts, and a picturesque downtown area lined with boutique shops, galleries, and a few cozy restaurants. The town's harbor is perfect for boating and fishing, with breathtaking views of the Chesapeake Bay. Sunrises in Lyndville are particularly stunning, often painting the sky in vibrant hues of orange, pink, and purple.

The town's relaxed pace and friendly community make it a perfect getaway for those looking to experience Virginia's coastal charm without the hustle and bustle of more tourist-heavy areas. Whether someone enjoys strolling along the beach, exploring nature trails, or enjoying fresh seafood at a local eatery, Lyndville offers a quintessential small-town beach experience.

If only we had a better coffee shop, I think, this town would be downright perfect.

As I walk, I enjoy the main street lined with small, independently owned shops and cafes, many housed in historic buildings with colorful facades and wooden signs. Flower boxes overflow with seasonal blooms, and there are benches where locals and visitors can sit and enjoy the sea breeze.

The shops offer a mix of local crafts, artisanal goods, and beach-themed souvenirs. At the corner are a vintage ice cream parlor with a striped awning, a bookstore with creaky wooden floors, and a family-run bakery with the smell of fresh pastries wafting out the door.

Street lamps glow softly this early in the morning, casting a golden light on the cobblestone streets. Just outside downtown, a small park provides a green space where families can gather, with a quaint fountain at the center.

The downtown area is just a short walk from the beach, where the sound of waves crashing can be heard in the background. The combination of charming architecture, local flavor, and proximity to the ocean make Lyndville feel like a hidden gem, a place where time slows down and the simple pleasures of life are easily found.

As I walk, I can't help but think about my challenges at work. Is my head not really in it enough to do the job? Are Jean and my teammates being too demanding? Or do I just have too much going on in my personal life that's getting in the way?

My mind flits back to the date with Bryan. I know I'm physically attracted to him and I had fun at the tapas restaurant with him over the weekend. But I really hardly know him at all. Our dates have been somewhat clouded with too much drinking, at least for him anyway, and that gives me pause. A guy who drives a passenger to a restaurant and then drinks so much he has to call an Uber…seems odd if not downright dangerous.

I wonder how much of a pattern this is versus just having a bad day. After all, Bryan is dealing with a lot of stress with his mom in the hospital.

And he's brand new in town so maybe he's still settling in? Dealing with some anxiety by self-medicating with alcohol?

For now, I'm going to look at Bryan's situation as a hopefully temporary reaction rather than an ongoing pattern, but I'll keep an eye on it for my own wellbeing.

And then my mind goes to my friendship with Ethan and how I'm starting to feel differently about him than I did in the past. More and more, I'm noticing his boy next door good looks and his athletic build. What's that all about? Am I actually becoming romantically attracted to Ethan or is it just the blossoming of our friendship and my deep gratitude for his support at work?

And once again, I tell myself I need to tread carefully because I don't want to end up hurting one of them by dating both men.

As I continue my stroll, I decide to set all of those thoughts aside and just breathe in the beauty of my town, the water, and the waves. The salt air acts as a calming agent for my mind and I find I can just let the swirling thoughts go for now and breathe. The waves crash and a gull calls overhead. I tune in to the sounds, sights, and smells around me and all too soon, arrive at my building to start the day.

I look up at the three story nondescript corporate headquarters and feel the reality of my work week come crashing back. The walk helped calm my mind, but it didn't take away my current work reality. I'm on a performance plan and could at any time be let go. I'm having difficulty keeping up with my work and the pace of the team for whatever reason.

And that all adds up to a fairly high level of anxiety each day when I walk into this bland building. Even when I'm trying my best and taking Jean's and the team's feedback to heart, I'm not confident I can meet expectations. This feeling of remorse and frustration for not being able to focus adds to the anxiety and makes it even harder to focus. It feels like an avalanche of anxiety picking up speed rushing down a hill.

Ethan's words come back to me at that moment. ""If it's right, it will work and if it's not, it won't." I take a deep breath, open the door and walk in, bracing myself for whatever will come my way this week.

Chapter 23

The workweek goes so-so, all things considered. My
performance meeting with Jean doesn't come with any surprises,
and I find myself feeling tentatively hopeful. But I'm still on a
warning status which gives me a constant sense of anxiety at
work. I agree to have lunch with Ethan (as a friend and
coworker, I remind myself) on Thursday and find I'm looking
forward to catching up with him. I want to hear all about his
work at the shelter, his challenges and progress with his ADHD.
And I even feel like I want to pick up the coffee shop business
plan conversation with him. I think of it kind of like a lottery
ticket, something fun to dream about for someday.

We decide to walk toward the beach and grab to-go meals
from the Mediterranean place on the way. I choose a vegetarian
sampler platter with an amazing spicy mixed vegetable salad,
hummus, warm fluffy pita, and a slightly spicy eggplant dip,
baba ganoush. Ethan has striped bass, pepper and onion skewers
with the pita, and a parsley infused tabbouleh. It all smells
divine.

A set of tables at the beach offers a view of the water with
the sun glinting off the waves.

"Guess what, Ethan. I think I'm ready to get back to our
coffee shop planning. Things have calmed down with my

parents and their health and at work. I get so psyched just thinking about it, even if I never do it, it's fun to dream. What do you think?"

"That's fantastic, Sophia. I agree it has been a lot of fun and I'm happy to pick it back up whenever you want."

We dig into our food, watch and listen to the waves, and enjoy the quiet time away from the office to recharge.

I'm thinking about how I could make this a reality…just for fun. Or maybe to distract myself from my work woes.

"If I could get a loan and/or maybe some grant money to get started, I believe I could do this. I think I would need to quit my job. But that wouldn't be such a bad thing, maybe. I like it, but I don't love it. I keep thinking how we all think our lives will go on forever, but the reality is…the reality."

"That's very true, Sophia. If we keep thinking about this as just a dream, it won't happen. But if we start to think about what would need to be true to make this work, I think we'd have a better shot."

"You're talking in the royal "we" sense, Ethan. Would you want to get into this as a partnership?"

"Quite possibly, Sophia. I'm in the same place you are with work. It's a fine job I have, but it's a job. Wouldn't it be amazing if we could spend every day closer to the beach, listening to the waves and the seagulls…serving people delicious coffee?"

"Yes, it would be amazing. Imagine every day we're smelling the tang of salt water in the air and the chocolate aroma of a fine Brazilian blend. How many more sections of the business plan do we need to get through before you think we could apply for a loan?"

"I'd say we're maybe 60% done, but we have some of the hardest parts to go. Like we talked about before, cash flow, projections and such. I have a decent head for numbers, so what if I just brainstorm a proposal and you can review it and see what you think? That way, you have something to react to rather than trying to drum it up in your head, if the financial side is something you don't enjoy."

"LOVE IT. And I'm happy to go work on some other sections of the plan. We can divide and conquer."

Ethan's eyes sparkle and he has a serene smile on his face. Then he looks up and to the side as though he's thinking deeply and trying to look at his thoughts.

"What are you thinking about now? You look all thoughtful."

"Mostly I'm thinking about the coffee shop dream. And, Sophia, I have to tell you I think you're an amazing person and I want you to be happy. I want you to be treated like the coffee queen you are. Or maybe you'd rather I call you coffee princess but coffee queen sounds better, don'cha think?"

"Yes, Coffee Queen, please call me that and that only from now on. I won't answer if you don't," I joke.

I'm not sure Ethan has shared everything he's thinking about. The sparkle in his eyes seems to go beyond excitement about a coffee shop. I wonder if he's starting to have more in depth feelings about me as I am about him. And I wonder about his mention of how I should be treated…is he referring to Bryan?

I bring myself back to the topic.

"How long do you think it will take you to work on the cash flow and financial projections for the business plan? I'll work on details of the marketing strategy and customer profiles and we can get back together and share notes."

"Maybe a week? I have a couple shifts at the humane society after work this week, but I can definitely work on it some over the weekend. Also I thought I heard that the city is giving out some kind of grant or stimulus money to encourage new small businesses to start up. I can do some research on that and see if there is some kind of application process, or how we might be able to tap into something like that."

"Wouldn't that be fantastic? A loan would be great, but add grant money and we'd have less to ask for from the bank and more importantly, money we would have to worry about paying back with interest."

"Yes, exactly. And it's good for the city, of course. The more people want to come here and spend money, the more taxes the city collects. It's a good cycle."

"I literally don't know what tourists do when they need a good cappuccino or macchiato. Do they drive twenty miles away? Do they bring their own espresso maker? I bet some tourists consider Lyndville for their vacation and then just decide, 'nah, no good coffee shops.' It's an important part of any city and especially a city that relies on tourism."

"Right, and that's a lot of the story we need to tell in our business plan, loan, and grant applications…is how we will be meeting a demand that is huge and for the most part untapped."

Ethan and I agree we'll get together the following week to look at our drafts. As we head back to work, I feel like I'm walking on a cloud. As we cross the street, Ethan puts a protective hand gently on my lower back and I feel a jolt of electricity. A zing of warmth spreads through my body.

Is it just all part of the excitement I'm feeling about the coffee shop dream becoming a reality? Or is there something more to how I'm feeling about Ethan? I realize I haven't thought for a minute about Bryan in the last several hours. Or has it been longer?

When I do think about Bryan, I realize I'm still quite attracted to him physically but something about him seems…just off.

I decide to just let those thoughts percolate in the back of my mind. I chuckle to myself at the coffee joke and head back to my real job.

Chapter 24

The first release of the coffee website is due out at the end of the week. The team has several late nights to get the initial development wrapped up and be prepared for the presentation to the client for feedback. I've worked closely with this client from the beginning to translate their vision for the site into designs. I feel both nervous and excited about the presentation. My job will be to lead the developers through the functionality and explain it to the client. It's a complex site so I start to develop a set of talking points on Monday when my cell phone rings with my mom's ringtone.

My mom doesn't call me at work often, so I have a sinking feeling when I answer.

"Hey Mom, what's up, is everything ok?"

"Yes and no, Sophia. I need to take your dad to the hospital. He's been throwing up for several hours now, and his regular doctor is worried about dehydration. He doesn't seem too worried about it overall, but I thought you'd want to know right away. It could be just a bug he picked up or food poisoning. I'm not sure if they'll do tests at the hospital or what, but we are headed there now."

I'm so torn about whether I should go with my parents to the hospital or keep working on my presentation. On the one hand, my mom seems calm and fine to drive Dad. And of course, I have this big deadline and this looming performance status at work. On the other hand, family is family and I want to be there for both my parents.

"Mom, do you need or want me to drive you or meet you there? I can leave here in ten minutes if you need me to." I decide to leave out the part about the presentation and the deadline to not sway my mom's answer.

"Oh, Sophia, that would be so helpful if it doesn't cause you too much grief. Having you there I think will help your dad feel better, and I know it will help me to have your company.

"But I don't want to disrupt your week. Is this a bad time?"

"I'll be fine. I'll bring my laptop and can work while we wait. There's always a lot of time waiting at a hospital, so I'll just get work done there."

"Oh, thank you so much, honey. I'll see you soon."

I power down my laptop and stop by Jean's office to let them know what's going on and how I plan to keep working on the client presentation. Jean gives me a concerned look and says "Do what you need to do, Sophia. I understand you need to be there for your family."

As I drive to the hospital, I keep thinking about the presentation and I miss the turn onto the highway leading to the hospital. Instead, I had been driving back home.

I'm frustrated I've wasted time. And it shows I'd rather be in my comfy, quiet apartment. Wishful thinking, I muse as I backtrack to get on the highway.

Sure enough, once we meet up in the emergency room waiting room, we're told the wait will likely be a couple hours before my dad will be seen.

My dad looks positively awful. His color is ashen, his cheeks look sunken and he has dark circles under his eyes. I hug him and ask what I can do to help him feel better.

"How about you go get me a pizza. Make that extra large with everything including anchovies," my dad jokes.

"EWWWWW, you wouldn't eat anchovies even if you didn't feel like crap, Dad. Who are we kidding?"

My dad smiles weakly and says "Yeah, maybe another time. You can hold my hand while I puke, how about that? Or keep my hair out of my face?"

My dad is nearly bald so I chuckle and realize I'm super glad he still has his sense of humor.

I try to do what I can to soothe him as they wait. I take turns with my mom getting small cups of ice chips from the cafeteria when he thinks he can take them. All plans of working on my presentation go out the window for the next several hours as we wait to be seen and get Dad headed in a better direction.

Once we finally see a doctor three hours later, we're told that yes, Dad will need to be admitted so they can administer IV fluids and they also want to check on some pain he's having in his stomach. He hadn't mentioned that part to me and my mind goes to all of the awful things that could be.

"Don't worry, Sophia," Dad says. "I'm a tough old goat, and I'm not ready to call it quits yet."

But of course, I do worry. The tests they want to run can't be done until late in the day and we won't hear any results for another day or two, at least. I call Jean to let them know I'll be at the hospital for the rest of the day, but that I'll keep working on the presentation here. I try to work and keep my mind off my dad's illness. But each time I get started, my mind keeps wandering back to horrible potential outcomes for my dad.

Plus, I feel guilty putting my focus on work when my dad is feeling so bad and my mom is beside herself with worry.

I finally tell myself today is only Monday. I still have three more days to prepare for this client presentation. I'm just going to set work aside for the rest of the day and be fully present with my parents. I spend the rest of the day doing just that.

I read a few chapters to my dad from the novel he brought. We play hangman to distract ourselves and to wile away the time.

By mid-afternoon, they've settled my dad into a hospital room with a view of the park across the street. They've administered anti-nausea drugs, and his color looks a little better.

With each passing hour of getting more fluids into him, his cheeks look less sunken and his spirits seem to rise. My mom is also perking up from the improvement in my dad. At 5:00, they wheel him out for his follow up testing. My mom and I wait in the hospital room for his return.

"Sophia, I can't thank you enough for being here today. I'm so glad he's starting to feel better and hopefully, this testing will uncover the issue and he'll be home in no time."

"I hope that too, Mom and I'm glad I was here with you today. We'll stay hopeful and try not to worry unless the doctors tell us we need to worry."

Chapter 25

I had another night of fitful sleep and strange dreams. I can't quite recall them but I know they have to do with my attempt at avoiding the fears I feel about my dad's illness and my stressful time at work.

On Tuesday morning, I checked in with my mom at the hospital and learned my dad was doing ok with the anti-nausea drugs and the IV fluids.

He's not much better or worse than he was at the end of the day before. Most importantly, the tests won't come back until late in the day, so I decide to go in to work. I know it's important to be present with the team, let Jean see I'm there and get a good…well better start on the presentation.

When I arrive at work, I head straight to my cubicle and get started with the slides. Not thirty minutes later, a building worker arrives to do some work in the conference room near my cube. I'm having a hard time keeping the momentum and focus when the worker's drill keeps starting and stopping. After another hour or so, a group of co-workers from the marketing department show up to use the conference room for a baby shower. Their excited chatter and exclamations of 'oooooooos and aaaawwws' at the cute gifts come through the thin walls loud and clear as I try desperately to continue to focus on my work.

Right around 10:30, Ethan pops his head over my cubicle wall and gives me one of his trademark adorable smiles and asks me to lunch.

"I would love to, Ethan, believe me, but I have this presentation due and am having a really hard time getting it done with all the distracting noises going on here today. And my dad is in the hospital for testing so I was there all day yesterday and am feeling pretty behind. I really should work through lunch."

"No problem, Sophia. How about I pick up lunch for you so you don't even have to leave your desk?"

"That would be amazing, Ethan. You're so awesome to think of that. You know how I can get so HANGRY when I miss a meal. My hunger plus anger combo packs a punch."

"I would be happy to. I was going to get sandwiches from the diner so I'll grab your favorite.

"Also, at the risk of telling you TMI, one of the things I find with my ADHD is I need a quiet place to get work done and my manager has helped me make that happen. I have noise canceling headphones that work for minor levels of noise and when I know the office is going to be noisy. Some days I am able to just work from home. Again not saying you have ADHD, just telling you my experience."

"Wow, yes, a quiet place sounds amazing today. I've really struggled this morning with the work happening in this conference room and this baby shower."

"Yeah, and maybe ask Jean for some suggestions. Jean seems like a good manager who would want to help you be as productive as possible. After all, that's best for everyone on the team."

"Once again, Ethan, you're a lifesaver. I'm going to go talk to Jean as soon as I finish this slide and see what they suggest. I have to be honest. So much of your experience with ADHD resonates with me. I really may need to consider getting tested. And like you told me before, it's not really about the diagnosis as much as figuring out what's helpful for my unique challenges."

I send an instant message to Jean to ask when they can chat face to face. Eleven-thirty, Jean will be done with their staff meeting and I can stop by then.

The next hour continues to be less than productive as the baby shower crowd wraps up the event and chats away as they file out of the conference room. I hear snippets of their conversation about whether or not my co-workers could possibly stand not knowing whether they were having a girl or a boy...reflections on the cool stroller they saw etc.

My anxiety ratchets up further as I realize nearly another ½ day has passed and I've made minimal progress on the presentation.

At exactly 11:30, I knock on Jean's door. Jean waves me in and invites me to sit.

I explain in more detail what's going on with my dad at the hospital and that I'll need to go back later in the day. Then I launch into the topic of the lack of quiet that has challenged my progress all morning.

Jean listens with an empathetic look on their face.

"Well, Sophia, you know we've agreed this team needs to be present in the office Tuesday through Thursday unless something serious arises, like the medical situation your dad has encountered. But it sounds as though your dad has stabilized today, right?"

"Yes, he's doing pretty well today. I'm not going to the hospital until around 4."

Jean continues. "So technically, I would be breaking or at least bending the rules if I allowed you to work from home today. But at the same time, I do see how that noise from the conference room would make it very difficult to get your work done, especially if you're extra sensitive to distractions. And considering your performance status, I'm sensitive to the optics either way."

Jean sighs and seems to be thinking.

"Since the best outcome for everyone is that the presentation is wonderful and goes without a hitch, I'm willing to bend the rules in this case. And we can tell the team your dad is still in the hospital, which is true. Go ahead and head home so you can work in a quiet environment."

I breathe a sigh of relief.

"Thank you, Jean. This means so much and I promise, promise, promise, pinky swear I'll get a ton done this afternoon before I head to the hospital."

I text Ethan to let him know how the conversation with Jean went and that I won't be needing that sandwich after all since I'll be heading home.

He texts back a thumbs up and, "Go kick some ass, Sophia!"

And I plan to.

Chapter 26

I work diligently through the afternoon on the coffee website presentation in the quiet of my apartment. I'm super interested in this company and what they're doing, and I find myself fully absorbed in the work. I'll start with the overall mission statement and home page design, emphasizing the partnership the company has with coffee growers in Peru, Brazil, and Rwanda. From there, on the product page, I'll highlight each of the top selling coffees from those countries. I've included a little snippet on why each of the countries is considered a model for fair trade.

For example, the product description for the Peruvian blend called Coop-peru highlights how many of the coffee farmers are part of cooperative societies. I'm so fully absorbed in my work, I almost forget about my dad's test results later today, thankfully.

Next I'll introduce the shopping cart page...

I startle at the sound of my mom's ringtone on my phone a little before 4:00. Oh wow, I totally lost track of time there for a bit.

"Mom, I'm sooooooo sorry, I lost track of time. I'll leave here in 5 minutes and that should get me there around 4:15."

I feel a stab of guilt and panic. I'm going to be late for this important medical appointment, and I didn't get as far as I should have with the shopping cart page talking points. Even though the industry stuff is cool, the shopping cart page is what will get them revenue, so that needs lots of emphasis. My anxiety meter is pegging…again…as I shut down my laptop.

"OK, thanks, Sophia. I really appreciate you being here, and I know it's hard when you're working. I think your dad would agree it will be good if we are together as a family when the test results come in. See you soon."

I rush to get out the door and leave my cell phone on the table by my laptop.

Luckily, I realize when I get in the car and can't turn on my favorite calming music playlist. I'm frustrated that I'm now in a major rush and forgetting things.

What the hell is wrong with me? I know how important this is but I got so focused on work I lost track of time. As I run upstairs to get my phone, I decide to bring my laptop just in case there's a lot more waiting at the hospital. When I get in my apartment and grab my phone, I have a feeling I'm still forgetting something. I realize as I'm driving that I forgot my laptop. Sh★t, sh★t,sh★t, I think.

When I arrive at my dad's hospital room, the doctor is just leaving. A feeling of embarrassment and dread washes through me. If this doctor brought bad news, I missed it and I'll have to ask my parents to repeat whatever the horrible news is. The doctor's expression is unreadable as she nods briefly and walks quickly out the door.

But as I walk in the room, I see my mom and dad's expressions are beaming. This must be good news. Phewwwwwwwww!!!!

"Well, good news, Sophia," my mom says. "The testing ruled out anything really bad like appendicitis or a bowel obstruction. They think it was just a nasty bug, maybe even norovirus that caused cramping and pain. But nothing that will require surgery or have long lasting effects."

My dad's face is still drawn and tired but he's obviously relieved. "I still feel like crap, but what a relief it's just a run of the mill bug."

"How long do you think they'll keep you in the hospital?"

"They'd like to keep me on IV fluids for another day, but I should be heading home tomorrow with some prescription anti-nausea drugs. I'll be ready for that anchovy pizza in no time, I hope."

I release a breath I didn't realize I was holding. My mind had been going to multiple dreadful scenarios as I drove to the hospital and during the walk to the room, but none of them will come to be. The good news also means I don't need to stay at the hospital for very long today and can get back to the coffee website presentation. I visit with my parents for another hour before my dad yawns and says, "I'm beat. I didn't sleep very well last night."

"No wonder. I should go, then." I hug them and walk out the door. As I turn the corner near the cafeteria, I nearly run into a tall, muscular guy.

I look up to see Bryan heading towards the elevator.

"Hey, Sophia, good to see you. Well maybe not good to see you here but…what's up? Why are you here?"

I briefly study his long lashes and stormy blue eyes as I tell Bryan all about my dad's illness and positive prognosis.

"And I feel the same, nice to see you but not at the hospital. How's your mom doing?"

"She's stable. They seem to have landed on some medications that help and she's been getting regular breathing treatments. I was just dropping something off for her, no big emergency or anything.

"I'm glad I ran into you. I was going to ask if you'd like to go out again this weekend. Maybe we can find another place with live music. That was fun."

"I would love to. I'll give you a couple of suggestions for places that have decent food and live music, and you can pick."

"Sounds good, I'm not picky. As long as they have a good bar." He winks.

"Sure, yes, they all do. Hey, I have to run. I have a big presentation later in the week, and I need to get back to it. I'll text you the places I come up with and see you Saturday."

I take a moment to appreciate his muscular forearms and biceps in his golf shirt before I hurry back to my car.

By the day of the presentation, I feel good about my progress and preparation, but anxious about the meeting. Although I know the design is solid, I realize how much is riding on this one brief slice of time to woo the client. I take a deep breath and head into the conference room where the team and the client group are gathering. My anxiety ratchets up as the start time comes near. Jean handles introductions of the development team and the client team as well as the agenda.

"I think you'll be pleased with the designs this team will present today and you'll be ready to move into full blown development. We've done some preliminary development to give you a good idea of the flow of the site. So our goal today is to make sure you're comfortable with the design and the flow and get the green light to move ahead. Sophia, I'll turn it over to you to do the honors."

I feel my heart rate increase, my mouth go dry, and my breathing become shallow as all eyes turn to me. The talking points I had prepared seem to have flown out of my head.

I can't believe this is happening…what is going on? I begin to talk in an impromptu way about the website, but I get sidetracked talking about the fair trade coffee industry. I can see the puzzled looks on the clients faces and the concerned looks on my teammates' faces.

"What Sophia means to say is she's highlighted the importance of fair trade on the product page," Jean adds. "But how about we start with the home page, Sophia, and go from there."

The rest of the hour-long meeting goes in a similar way.

Each time the floor is turned over to me, I feel a rising panic and despite my preparation, I ramble and lose track of the key things I had planned to highlight.

At the close of the meeting, the client says, "What we've seen looks pretty good when we put it all together. But we'll need some time to regroup before we agree to move ahead. Jean, I'll get back to you on Tuesday next week. Thank you all for your time."

I feel like a zombie as I leave the conference room. I can see Jean and the client lead talking in quiet tones and Jean glancing at me as they talk. It's 4:30 so I pack up my laptop and head for home.

Chapter 27

I feel nauseous on my drive home. I replay the feeling of panic that set in and totally hijacked my brain throughout the presentation and erased all of my careful preparation. The worst part is I truly can't think of anything I could have done to be any more prepared, so why and how did my brain short circuit like that?

Once I reach my apartment, I've decided to make every effort to set my workday disaster aside. It's Friday and I have the weekend ahead. I may as well live it up a little.

I text Amira and ask if she'd like to head out to dinner. Two seconds later, I receive a "Hell Yeah" GIF with Snoop Dog dancing in response. Despite my crappy mood, I crack up at that. We agree to meet at Moma's Tapas Bar at 6 for a light dinner, and hopefully, a good band.

When I see Amira, a sense of relief washes over me. I'm so glad to have my friend and sounding board back in town. We hug and settle in to decide on food. Amira suggests some new items on the menu; blistered peppers with mozzarella, olive oil, and sea salt, mixed seafood hand pies, and a grazing platter of veggies.

"Hand pies, that sounds dirty," I tease.

Amira laughs. "They're little individual pizzas. I think you knew that and you're messing with me."

"Well yes, that's accurate."

"Tell me about your week," Amira says.

"Oh, jeez, it's been a week."

I sigh. On one hand, I don't want to spend the whole evening wallowing in my work woes, but on the other hand, I know Amira will listen and probably have good ideas for handling my reactions and emotions about it.

I start by telling Amira all about my dad's medical scare, and I quickly get to the happy result part of the story.

"Oh thank goodness!" Amira exclaims. "Send them both my love."

"Will do. On top of that, I had a huge presentation at work, and I managed to mess it up big time. I really tried my best to be ready for it. I prepared great slides and talking points to go along with it. But when the time came, my mind froze. You would think I was facing a firing squad rather than a roomful of clients. My heart was pounding, my mouth went dry, and everything I had prepared to say flew out of my head."

"Oh, crap, Sophia, that sucks. I'm so sorry to hear that. Honestly it doesn't sound unusual, considering the pressure you've been under. Your brain went into caveman, well, cavewoman, fight or flight mode. Not to go all psychology-ee on you, but the part of the brain that handles fear is called the amygdala. And for some people, myself included, our amygdales get all fired up sometimes and send us into a panicked state for no real good reason. We actually want our amygdales to be able to hijack our brains and skip over the processing steps if something dangerous happens, like a gunshot.

"You know I have anxiety, and I'm getting much better at managing situations which used to make me super anxious. I'm just now learning some new breathing techniques, and talk about it each week with my therapist to sort through what triggers my overachieving amygdala and why I get anxious."

"But anyway, back to what's going on with you. What did the client say? What did Jean say?"

"Ugggh, we left it in an awkward place because the meeting was at the end of the week. The client is going to get back to us, and I haven't really had a chance to debrief with Jean yet."

Amira's brow wrinkles and she makes a sad face.

"Well double sh*t on a shingle, Sophia. I think this calls for some dancing to release your negative energy. Speaking of dancing, what's up with Bryan? Has he called? Are you going out again?"

"Yes. Actually, I ran into him at the hospital earlier this week when I was there for my dad. He asked me out again this weekend."

Amira squeals with excitement. Her brown eyes sparkle and she twirls a curly lock of already curly hair around her finger.

"Oh my gosh, I can't wait to hear about your date. That guy is gorgeous. How do you not just stare at him the whole time you're out? I bet other women watch him the whole time you're out together."

"You're right." I laugh. "Not just women; the guy is so handsome that I think the whole world can't help but stare at him."

Our food arrives and while it looks delicious, I feel a wave of nausea swell up as the waiter sets the plates down. That's odd, I think.

But I guess I'm still thinking more about work in the back of my brain than I realized and it's making me queasy.

Amira digs into her food and I start to nibble at it.

"Enough about my drama, Amira, tell me about your week."

"Not a lot to tell, Sophia. I'm still getting adjusted to Eastern Standard time, so I'm up at the butt crack of dawn and exhausted by 7:30PM. I'm trying to stay awake a little later each night and hopefully will wake up a little later each day. It's working ok, but when I have a late night at work, I'm really dragging."

"I made a photo album of my favorite food experiences from France. Let me show you."

Amira fires up her photo album and launches into a lengthy presentation of baguettes, olives, and cheeses in various stunning French locations.

I once again find myself fighting a wave of nausea and puzzle why this would be.

I would normally be super excited for the French food tour but tonight, I just feel sick to my stomach.

Resources

Cleveland Clinic Overview of Amygdala

https://my.clevelandclinic.org/health/body/24894-amygdala

Chapter 28

My dreams that night are full of terrifying monsters and being terrorized by some nameless faces chasing me. I can't remember them as vividly as my under the sea dream, but I don't feel rested on Saturday morning. I know my mind is working overtime in the background about my awful presentation experience from Friday. I'm desperately trying to set those thoughts aside for the weekend and look forward to the downtime, but my brain is not cooperating. I feel exhausted and I have dark circles under my eyes. This isn't the best look for my date tonight with Bryan. Hopefully some artful makeup artistry will help…and maybe a nap later.

I spend the morning doing my normal Saturday errands, cleaning, and laundry, and head over to my parents' house for lunch. My dad seems to have mostly recovered from his stomach bug and trip to the hospital and eats well. He looks a little thinner and tired still, but that's to be expected, I think.

I decide not to tell them about my awful work presentation, not because I think they would be upset, but because I don't want to talk about it for now.

In the afternoon, I find I have a couple hours on my hands and decide to text Ethan to see if he's at the humane society. I enjoy seeing the cats, and I know he sometimes volunteers there on weekends.

A gif comes back almost immediately with a crowd of cats milling around a person's legs and his response, "Yes, you guessed it. I'm here now. Want to come meet me? There's a litter of four kittens in all colors of the rainbow."

I respond with a thumbs up and, "See you soon."

As I drive to the humane society, I decide I'll tell Ethan about my Friday panic attack. Maybe just telling someone else besides Amira will help me feel better.

When I arrive, I find Ethan in a brightly lit, glass enclosed room surrounded by eight kitty 'condos' which house the cats ready for adoption. They each have their own separate enclosures with a place for napping, a few toys, their food and water, and of course, their litter boxes. Ethan is playing with a large, orange male cat with a wand toy. I crack up as Ethan swings the toy and the cat jumps at it.

"That's a pretty good vertical leap height."

"Yes, Sophia, meet Mr. Orangu. I think that's short for an orangutan and because he's orange. They don't really know any of his history as far as who owned him. A good Samaritan saw him in the neighborhood and brought him in. He's 5 years old and can be a bit shy at first, but he'll warm up over time, so go slow and just offer your hand."

I sit on the floor and watch Ethan and Mr. Orangu play with the wand toy some more and after a few minutes, the cat walks over to me and bumps his head on my leg.

"That's a good sign, go ahead and pet him on the head, but not on his back yet."

I do, and Mr. Orangu puts his head up for scratches on the chin. He starts to purr and roll his head so my scratches hit exactly where he wants them. He shows me a patch of white fur on his chin.

"I hope he gets adopted soon." Ethan looks a little sad.

"He's going to make a great pet for someone, but older cats usually take longer to find a home. Speaking of cats that will get adopted soon, come meet the kittens."

Ethan entices Mr. Orangu back to his enclosure with a tasty treat and leads me to a corner condo which houses the kittens. I see four tiny fluffy balls of fur. One kitten is orange, one black, there's a tabby, and a white with tabby splotches sleeping together in a cardboard box with a blanket.

"They're not allowed on the floor yet because they're so young, but you can pet them in here and pick them up if you'd like."

I pet each of their soft, warm bodies and find myself relaxing. The stress of my previous week floats away as I enjoy the thrum of their tiny purring and adoring looks.

After they seem to have had their fill of petting and are dozing off to sleep again, Ethan and I take the rest of the cats out of their enclosures and play with them and pet them.

"This is a wonderful thing you do, Ethan. I'm sure the cats appreciate getting out and you're helping socialize them to humans."

Ethan smiles. "I get as much out of it as they do. I truly believe the purring sound of cats is a form of therapy for me. There's probably some science to it since a purring cat generally means we're safe. And of course, I have to exercise my less than stellar planning muscles to plan how I can get here around work. So it's a win-win, I'd say. "

"So, how's your dad doing? How did the rest of your week go?"

I recap the testing and my dad's return home and then I hesitate. Do I really want to tell him about the work debacle? I decide yes and launch in. As I talk, Ethan nods and gives me sympathetic looks as the story unfolds. He's looking deeply into my light brown eyes and seems to be listening not just with his ears but with his whole body.

When I finish my sad tale, Ethan wraps his arms around me and I realize I've started to tear up. I cry on Ethan's shoulder for a few minutes and when I feel cried out, I pull away and dab my eyes with a tissue.

"I don't know what to say, Sophia, other than that ultra, double, triple sucks. I can totally relate, too. I've found a few things that will trigger my anxiety monster and had that 'deer in headlights' feeling, even after I did everything I could to be ready. Is there anything I can do?"

"Not that I can think of, Ethan, just listening and letting me blubber was exactly what I needed. Oh, and introducing me to Mr. Orangu and the kittens, that helped too."

Ethan chuckles. "Well anytime you need feline therapy, you're welcome to come in here.

"This place is always full of soft, pettable ESAs."

"What's that? ESAs?"

"Emotional Support Animals. Lots of people with mental and or physical disabilities find the presence of a pet can relieve their symptoms. They're not service animals, exactly, it's more just being with them helps relieve symptoms, like anxiety.

"And they aren't considered pets when it comes to housing. People with ESAs don't have to pay the steep fees apartments sometimes charge for a pet."

"Wow, that's super cool. Maybe I need to bring Mr. Orangu to my next presentation. It would be great. I can wave his paws around to emphasize a point."

At that, Ethan starts to full belly laugh. Between giggles, he says "You can put his paw on the screen where the most important points of each slide are."

Pretty soon, we're both laughing our asses off and coming up with ways Mr. Orangu can help with the presentation, including advancing the slides when I point to him.

"But how will he use the clicker?" I giggle.

I soon realize it's time to head home and get ready for my date with Bryan.

"I can't tell you how much this has helped, Ethan. Just listening and letting me babble, and then crafting this brilliant, bullet proof plan to bring my ESA Mr. Orangu to my next presentation. It will be brilliant."

"I'm happy to help, Sophia, and always here for you."

Chapter 29

As I drive home from the humane society, exhaustion hits me like a wave. My lack of sleep is catching up. But I resolve to make a cappuccino when I get home to perk me up for my date with Bryan. The thought of looking into his stormy blue eyes, his wavy rich brown hair, and appreciating his muscular physique will keep me plenty awake.

I do my best to take the attitude of "fake it 'til you make it". Even though I don't feel lively, I apply makeup to make me look brighter. A sweep of bronzer, some light concealer for those pesky under eye circles and shimmering accents on my eyes make me feel better...at least 20 percent better, anyway.

I make myself a cappuccino using the fancy beans I bought online. The moment the fresh, earthy scent of coffee beans wafts through the air from my grinder, I feel more awake. As the hot water meets the grounds, the rich aroma intensifies, filling the space with a mix of roasted nuts, chocolate, and subtle fruity notes.

When I taste the coffee, the scent enhances its flavors, creating a harmony between smell and taste of the light, bright blend. The warmth of the cup in my hands deepens the sense of comfort and satisfaction.

Although the coffee smells fantastic and the warmth feels amazing on this cool fall day, I find my stomach feels a bit queasy afterward. Hmmm, maybe this blend is too acidic, I think.

Bryan picks me up a few minutes past 6 and we head out to dinner at the sandwich shop and plan to go to one of the popular beach bars afterward.

Bryan looks as handsome as ever, and I wonder how a guy can have such thick dark lashes. It seems entirely unfair. He's wearing a cornflower blue polo shirt that compliments his eyes.

At the sandwich shop, Bryan orders an Italian sub packed with salami, ham, turkey, and a smoky provolone. I decide on a tuna sub with roasted tomatoes, zucchini, and portobello mushrooms smothered with a basil sauce, and buttery mozzarella. Although the shop itself is a food truck, they've set up a pleasant seating arrangement with folding canvas chairs and brightly colored beach umbrellas. My mind wanders to my own coffee shop business idea, and I idly consider asking the shop owners where they got the furniture and how much it cost.

"...I couldn't believe I saw that bird. It's a lifer for me."

I shake myself back to the moment and realize Bryan had started into a story about his birding adventures while I had been daydreaming.

"I'm sorry, can you please tell me again where you were and the more common name of the bird?" I inwardly hope that question will cover up the fact that I entirely missed what he said in the first place.

Bryan looks puzzled and says "I think American Oystercatcher is the common name, and it was at the preserve up north, across the bridge where the sand juts out into the ocean."

"Wow, that's so cool! Congratulations."

Bryan tells me more about his birding ventures for the week and about all the books he's read. As he talks, I become more tired and my queasiness starts to blossom into full blown nausea. I don't eat even a third of my sandwich before I ask for a to-go container. I also find myself noticing Bryan hasn't yet asked me anything about my week. But I don't mind all that much, since I'm not feeling my best.

Once we get to the beach bar, Bryan asks what I'd like to drink. I ask for a ginger ale, hoping it will settle my stomach. He comes back to the table with two margaritas and the ginger ale.

"Since you're not drinking, would you mind being our designated driver tonight?"

"Oh sure, no problem."

The band starts up and we have a hard time hearing each other past that point. Bryan finishes off his margaritas and asks me if I'd like to dance. I can't imagine dancing to the current music selection and I figure his margaritas have put him in the right frame of mind, while I'm entirely sober. I agree but the minute I start to sway to the beat, a round of dizziness overtakes me. I realize I'm going to be sick and run to the restroom just in time.

Afterward, I splash cold water on my face and brush my teeth with the portable toothbrush I keep in my purse. I feel slightly better but know I'm going to have to end the date early. I guess I probably picked up the stomach bug from my dad earlier in the week. If I'm right, I know I'm in for a long next couple of days.

Bryan looks sympathetic and disappointed when I tell him what I think is going on.

He's ordered another drink and says "Let me just finish this and we'll take off."

"I'm so sorry to have to cut our date short. I've been looking forward to it all week. But it looks like Dad passed on more than just his love this week."

"It happens, Sophia. We'll have another chance, I hope. Unless you're just always a party pooper like this."

I manage a weak chuckle in response. "Yeah, no, I'm usually tons of fun but not today."

Chapter 30

Saturday night into Sunday morning, I'm sick about every hour. Eventually, I have nothing left in my stomach, but my body still goes into vomiting mode somehow. I think I may be running a fever and I'm getting weaker from dehydration and exhaustion. I realize no one but Bryan knows I'm sick because I didn't text anyone when it all started on Saturday. I try to sleep between rounds of heading to the bathroom and eventually curl up on the bathroom floor. The silver lining to all of this, I think in a haze, is this has temporarily taken my mind off my work woes.

Around mid-morning, I check my phone. My mom, Amira, and Ethan have texted me. I'm too tired to respond and I go back to attempting sleep in between rounds of retching.

At noon, I'm roused by a knocking on the door. I can't muster the energy to get up and call out, "I'm sick, who's there?"

"It's Ethan, I'm coming in. What's your door code?"

"You don't want to come in, this is too contagious."

"Sophia, I'm coming in. I'll wash my hands and take care of myself, but this is NOT up for debate."

Ethan punches in the door code and lets himself in. He finds me on my bathroom floor looking ashen and out of it.

He grabs a pillow and a red fleece blanket from my bed and brings them to me. Next, he grabs a soft washcloth and gently washes my face.

"Mmmmm, that cool cloth feels nice."

He gets another washcloth and gives it to me to put on my forehead.

"OK, Sophia, we need to get you into an urgent care place. I know you don't feel up to it, but I'll drive you and they can help you feel better, I promise."

"Ethan, I don't want to get you sick too."

"I'll wear a mask in the car if it will help but also...NOT up for debate. You don't have to suffer through this to this degree. You can also wear a mask in the car if it will make you feel better."

"I don't think anything can make me feel better at this point, I think I'm dying."

"I'm sure it feels that way. Now let's get you to the car."

Ethan puts his arm around me and helps me walk slowly and carefully to the car. Once I'm seen at urgent care, I'm given an injection of an anti-nausea drug. They want to see if they can stop the vomiting long enough for me to keep down fluids or if I'll need IV fluids.

"This is like déjà vu all over again with my dad's experience this week. The fluids made him feel like a new man. I already feel a little better. I'm going to try those ice chips."

Ethan stays with me at the urgent care facility for the next hour and a half, chatting with me to keep my mind off my illness and bringing me ice chips. They finally release me with instructions to come back in or go to the emergency room if I'm not able to keep fluids down.

As we drive back home, I realize I haven't heard from Bryan at all yet. That seems odd, considering he knew how badly I was feeling when we parted ways on Saturday. And on the other hand, Ethan showed up to save the day, even though we didn't have plans.

"Ethan, why did you come to my place today? We didn't have plans I'm forgetting about did we? Were we supposed to work on the coffee shop stuff today?"

"No, you didn't stand me up for a date." Ethan jokes. "I was just going to leave you a copy of the draft work I'd done so you can see how things look. Sometimes it's easier to look at a printout than a screen."

My mood lifts at the thought of my coffee shop.

"That's so sweet of you. And how do things look?"

"Are you sure you're up for shop talk now?"

"Yes, Ethan, give me the scoop. It's keeping my mind off my nausea and lifting my spirits. What did you find out?"

"Well in the good news department, Lyndville wants to encourage small business start ups, and so they've got several things that will be helpful to you. Financially speaking,

Lyndville has grants and tax incentives to help you get started. They also have a business incubation offering."

"Huh? Business incubation offering? Sounds like I'm a chicken, what's that all about?"

"The business incubation department provides mentors and office space for small business owners to get advice and a place to work as they start up the business. They can also help with lots of other things if you qualify, like helping you with site selection, marketing, infrastructure, and even administrative assistance."

"Wow, who knew all of this was a thing in Lyndville?"

"They're trying to get the word out, but it's not been...I'll use air quotes here "advertised" because it's just getting started. Maybe they need an incubator for their incubator. Anyway, the info is pretty easy to find on the city's website. So I made some projections and scenarios for you to think about. If you got this much in grant funding and that much in loans, this would be your income stream. I also did some thinking about scenarios if you wanted to start small with a coffee cart structure rather than a full blown shop. Obviously the expenses are different if you were to rent a space in an existing building or buy a food truck and get it ready for coffee service."

"This is so exciting! So you really think it's possible for me to get some of the funding to get this started?"

"I do, Sophia. And you have the benefit of having a good knowledge of the coffee industry from the project you're doing now. And you have roots here in Lyndville. You know the town, you know the people, your family lives here. All those things will be positive for your chances."

I take a deep breath. I'm feeling better in so many ways. I had started the day curled up on my bathroom floor being sick and feeling alone. I was low key worried about my job in spite of the illness distracting me. And now I feel physically better from the anti-nausea meds and the fluids I'm able to keep down. But more importantly, I feel supported and hopeful about my dream becoming a reality.

Chapter 31

I don't feel like doing anything but sleeping for the rest of the day on Sunday. Ethan drops me off in the afternoon and I go straight to bed. I wake up around 11PM thirsty, but not feeling like I'm ready for any food yet. I drink two glasses of water and go back to bed.

Monday morning, I feel weak as a kitten. I wonder about that saying, since the kittens I saw at the humane society were anything but weak…tumbling over each other and jumping around in their enclosure. I shake my head away from the wandering path it's gone down and resolve to call Jean. I'm dreading speaking with Jean after Friday. And I know being out today will be a poor reflection on me but it can't be helped. I decide I'll offer to share the urgent care records with Jean if it will help to show I really am sick.

I take a deep breath and dial. Jean picks up on the first ring.

"Good morning, Sophia."

"Good morning, Jean. I wanted to first apologize for Friday. I was well prepared, but I let the team down. I can't explain what happened, my mind just froze up. It was a poor reflection on all of us, but of course, most of all me."

I pause and wait for a response.

"I appreciate your apology and ownership of the situation, Sophia. I don't think we should talk about it over the phone, though."

On some level, meeting with Jean face to face sounds terrifying to me, but I tend to agree. We should discuss this more in person. And now I have to let Jean know I won't be in this morning.

"OK, I understand. Let's talk more when we can meet in person. Unfortunately, that can't be this morning. I won't be in the office because I caught that awful stomach bug, probably from my dad. I spent most of yesterday in urgent care. Today I need to rest. And I may still be contagious, so it's better for the whole team if I stay home."

Jean sighs out a long breath.

"I see. Keep me posted and I hope you're feeling better soon."

"I will, thank you Jean."

I drink a cup of ginger tea and go back to bed. When I wake up around 11, I'm finally feeling the tiniest bit hungry. I check my phone and see texts from Amira, my mom, Ethan, and Bryan, checking on how I'm doing. I give each of them an update and go to the kitchen and make some toast. I briefly wonder how things are going at work with me out. I wonder if the team is trying to do damage control with the coffee client.

Maybe it's better I'm not there, I think. Then I go back to bed and sleep for three more hours.

When I wake up late in the afternoon, I see a text from Amira saying she's coming over with some homemade chicken noodle soup and a loaf of crusty bread. Suddenly, I'm ravenous. I send Amira a gif with a hangry hippo and tell her to hurry up.

Amira quickly responds with a thumbs up and, "I'll be there in twenty minutes."

When Amira arrives with the soup and bread, I give her a hug, thank her, and start right in on the soup.

"So catch me up on everything. You've been busy."

I realize I've only briefly updated Amira on my work debacle, my date with Bryan, and my trip to the urgent care with Ethan. As I recount my last few days, Amira listens and nods and looks thoughtful.

"Wow, that's a lot to unpack. No wonder you got sick, your poor immune system is probably defenseless from the work stress. Are you afraid you're going to lose your job?"

I tell Amira about my conversation with Jean earlier in the day.

"Realistically, yes, I am afraid of losing my job, considering Jean saying we need to talk in person. That sounds pretty ominous."

"I'm sorry to hear that Sophia. Of course, it's not unusual for people to be let go from a job, but that doesn't make it feel better."

"Exactly. I can tell myself that…it's just not a fit or whatever I want to rationalize. But it still sucks. I actually like this job but I've just had such a hard time lately getting it done. I'm actually starting to think I have ADHD, anxiety, or both.

"And that's not an excuse, that's just the reality…maybe."

"Maybe you're right, Sophia. Have you ever been tested for ADHD?"

"No, I didn't actually even know much about it until Ethan and I started chatting about it recently. I thought of it as an illness kids outgrow. More and more adults are being diagnosed with it nowadays, and particularly women.

"We have a tendency to hide the symptoms well, considering societal pressure to follow the rules."

"Well, that may be something to consider…get tested and see where that takes you. That could help you with accommodation at work, medications, and just feeling better about the fact that you have a very real illness. Just like you stayed home today…no one questions a physical illness, but many people don't think of a mental illness in the same way."

"Good advice, Amira. Thank you."

"Now tell me more about this date with Bryan. Are there sparks there?"

I think for a moment. "Sparks, yes. I'm physically attracted to him. But…I don't know if we're compatible otherwise. He's a nice enough guy, but it seems like he can't relax unless he's had a few drinks. And that's a red flag for me. He also didn't check in with me on Sunday…another red flag. He knew I was ill and didn't text me until Monday."

Amira furrows her brow. "Agree, Sophia. It doesn't sound like he's putting you on a pedestal and that's what you deserve. Don't settle for anything less."

"Amira, you are full of good advice today. You should charge for it…or write a newspaper column."

Amira laughs. "You're my best friend, Sophia. I want the best for you. Keep in mind, it's easy to look at someone else's life from the outside and tell them what to do. So actually, I'm just being nosy and bossy. And while I'm telling you what to do, I think you should really think about dating Ethan."

I smile at my friend. "I can see why you would say that. He's really been such a strong supporter for me. And he *is* super cute in an all American guy kinda way."

Amira hugs me. "So there we have it. Don't be too hard on yourself if you lose your job, dump Bryan, and start dating Ethan. Amira has spoken."

"Wise woman you are, Amira."

Chapter 32

Throughout the rest of Monday night, I feel better and better. The soup and bread gave me a burst of strength, and I'm able to keep down plenty of water. Despite an undercurrent of dreading the next workday, I sleep relatively well since I'm no longer nauseous and exhausted.

When I arrive at work, I start to catch up on emails, meetings, and instant messages. I have a meeting invite from Jean at 8:30, and I find I'm relieved. Rip the bandaid off, I think. When I arrive for the meeting, our Human Resources representative is also in Jean's office.

"Oh, sorry to interrupt. I can wait until you're done."

"Actually, Sophia, Jim will be joining the meeting today."

My stomach lurches. I hope I don't have to jump up and leave the meeting to be sick. But I know it's probably nerves, not the return of my stomach bug.

"I see."

I had started to be honest with myself about how my challenges got in the way of my job performance. I would lose track of time, forget important tasks, and struggle to stay organized. And dropping the ball on the presentation on Friday appears to be the last straw.

"Sophia, you know I appreciate all your hard work, but we've had too many issues lately," my boss Jean said gently. "I'm afraid we have to let you go."

"If you'd like me to go over the exact issues, I'd be happy to give you those details. And I apologize for the pain this will cause and jumping right in. But I don't think it will be helpful to delay or dance around it.

"Would you like me to go on and /or do you have any questions or comments?"

"Go on, I agree, let's get this over with."

"You can start a transition plan to Charles. He'll be taking over your duties. Your last day will be at the end of next week. We'll tell the team you're leaving to pursue new opportunities, and it's up to you how much you tell them about this conversation. Jim will go over the particulars on extending your health insurance, filing for unemployment, and so on.

"You will be receiving severance pay, which is usually not the case when we let someone go for performance reasons. But I can see you made a good faith effort, and so I've asked Jim to include that as part of your separation package."

"I understand and I don't need you to go over the issues, Jean. We've been meeting and covering them for a few weeks now, so that's not necessary. I do very much appreciate you advocating for a severance package for me. I did try, believe me I did.

"If it's ok, I'm going to leave the building for a few minutes to process."

"Of course, Sophia. I'm truly sorry it came down to this.

"This is the part of my job I don't enjoy. I had hoped we could get through to a better place but that unfortunately didn't happen quickly enough. The issues you've been having had a negative effect on your teammates and could cost us the engagement with the coffee client. I hope you understand this is not personal, it's business.

"I wish you the best and I hope you overcome whatever was holding you back in this job."

I left the building in tears, feeling lost and overwhelmed. I walked toward the ocean and sat on a bench with tears streaming down my cheeks. I wondered what I would do next. As if sensing my distress, Ethan appeared, concern etched on his face.

"Sophia, what's wrong? I saw you run out of the building," he asked, sitting down beside me.

"I lost my job," I replied, my voice breaking. "I…I just couldn't keep up."

Ethan took my hand in his, his touch reassuring. "I'm so sorry, Sophia. But this doesn't define you. You're incredibly talented and passionate. We'll find a way through this together."

I take a shaky breath. Although I'm devastated by the news, I feel something else…relief that this chapter of my life is coming to a close. I'd been carrying the burden of anxiety from my performance status on my shoulders for what seems like a very long time. And now, that burden was lifted. I'm going to be free to move on to the next chapter of my life.

"There is a silver lining or two in all of this. Jean was kind enough to negotiate severance pay for me. And I get unemployment. Not that I want to make that a long term solution, but I'll be able to pay my bills, anyway."

"That is good news. In fact, if I'm being entirely honest, I'm more than a little jealous. So while I'll have to keep slaving away in our boring corporate box, you'll be walking the beach, feeling the wind in your hair, and planning to take over the Lyndville coffee scene with your new business."

"You're right, Ethan. I'll still meet you for lunch, and I'll be able to make way more progress on the business plan with the free time I'm about to have. We should probably get back to the office. I need to start my transition plan to Charles. I like the sound of that…transition plan. I'm transitioning.

"What's that saying about doors closing?" I ask.

Ethan responds, *"When one door closes, another opens; but we often look so long and so regretfully upon the closed door that we do not see the ones which open for us."*

"Yes, that's the one. How do you know the whole thing by heart?"

"I think I told you I use quotes to get in the right frame of mind and that's one of my favorites. Fernando de Rojas offered that and it's one I live by. It's so true. I used to dwell a lot on failures and things I couldn't achieve but finally realized that's a complete waste of time. Fernando was a smart dude."

"I spent a lot of time feeling sorry for myself with my ADHD diagnosis, thinking about all the things I wasn't going to be able to do. But that's "closed door" thinking. I can do anything I want in life. Some things are harder for me because of my ADHD, so I need to accept that...give myself more time, get to a quiet place, or whatever I need.

"And I actually believe my ADHD gives me an advantage in some ways. I can be a strategist...I love to start stuff, even though I don't like to finish it. I sometimes feel as though my brain can actually think about multiple things at the same time, more so than so called normal people can.

"And maybe I'm just blowing smoke up my assss...actually, but you get where I'm going."

"Ethan, I can't thank you enough for your support and this pep talk. Let's head back to corporate box land so I can hammer out that transition plan."

"Can I give you a hug?"

"That would be lovely. Please do."

Ethan's hug lasts slightly longer than needed under the circumstances, but I don't mind. I'm enjoying his strength and his scent, today a blend of warm spices and citrus. I feel surprisingly calm and happy as we walk back to work.

Chapter 33

I sense my teammates want to know what happened in the meeting with Jean and Jim. I decide to simply tell them I'm leaving and the timeline for my transition. They don't need to know that I've been fired, though they likely know or will figure it out. As Ethan said, this job doesn't define me.

I start putting together a transition plan for Charles but at the same time, I find myself wanting to get started on finding a new job. I go into my LinkedIn profile and tweak it. While I'm logged in, I notice several requests to connect. I also see some suggestions for connections and submit a few of those. Wait...I'm off track, I think.

I decide to meet with Charles to get clear on what he knows and what he needs to know. Charles has a nice template I can follow which outlines the meetings he will need to take over, upcoming deliverables, dates, and so on.

I go back to my desk, fully intending to complete the template. But I realize I have several things due this week and meetings to prepare for. Charles won't be ready to lead any of those so soon. So I work on all of them, sort of, in between jumping into my job search. I spend nearly an hour that day perusing Indeed and Monster job sites to see what openings I might apply for. Then I realize I need to update my resume and do some work on that. As I jump from task to task, I feel anxious that I've not completed any of them.

The next few days continue in a similar manner with jumping between meetings, deliverables, and working with Charles. I make updates to my resume and connections on LinkedIn. In some ways, this is even harder than trying to focus on just getting my job done.

On Wednesday, I go over to my parents house for dinner. I'm dreading telling them about my work situation, but I know I shouldn't put it off. Bad news doesn't age well like wine.

When I arrive, my mom seems harried to get the meal ready.

"How can I help?"

"Nothing I can think of, honey, I just lost track of time to get started and then had a hard time finding the ingredients in the freezer. I swear your dad buys three of everything when he goes to the store and then forgets what he already bought since it gets buried under the last round of things we haven't eaten yet. He has other wonderful qualities, of course, but keeping a neat freezer isn't one of his fortes."

"Relatable. I do that with clothing sometimes; when I can't find my navy cardigan, I buy another one...only to find my navy cardigan a week later."

Once we sit down to dinner, I tell my parents about being fired. I tell them how the presentation last week was the 'straw that broke the camel's back' and how I really tried to do my best but just struggled. I also tell them I'll be getting severance, filing for unemployment, and getting extended health care, so I'm going to be ok financially. And through it all, I manage not to cry. Maybe I'm cried out.

My parents nod sympathetically and, thankfully, don't seem terribly concerned.

"You know, Sophia, I had a similar experience in my early twenties..." says my dad. "I'm trying to think of the name of my boss at the time...doesn't matter. Anyway, I left the company before they fired me. I probably should have stuck it out but I was just really embarrassed that I couldn't keep up. Other people with the same job seemed to be able to stay on top of the details way better than I could."

"Dad, you never told me about that. When we talked before, you told me about the metrics story and the boss you had to set straight."

"Well, I didn't want to sound like a negative Nancy...or a negative Ned, I guess, by jumping right in with that story.

"So I went for the one with the happy ending."

"Ahhh, I see. Well, I am starting to see this as a happy ending, believe it or not. My not being able to stay out ahead of the team and support them was really bringing me down. I put a lot of stress on myself. Well, and of course, the team did need me to deliver, and I couldn't so I was letting them down. The person I'm transitioning to, Charles, is picking things up quickly and I think he'll do a great job. So everything is in good hands with Charles."

★★★

At the end of the week, Jean puts a meeting on my calendar as a transition touch base. They've invited Charles and want to walk through the transition plan.

Charles and I start to talk through all of the meetings they've had and what Charles is taking over next week.

Jean says "I'm glad it looks like you're making progress, but Sophia, I really need you to put all the details in the transition plan. Charles is very smart, but you can't expect him to remember everything without documenting it. You need to write down the meetings and times, the locations of the documents and so on."

"I will do that, Jean. Charles gave me a really nice template to complete, but I just haven't gotten to filling it out yet. It's been a busy week."

Jean nods. "Charles, you can take off. I just have a couple of last items to cover with Sophia. Thanks for your time."

Jean hands me an envelope after Charles leaves.

"This is your severance. I tried to help as much as I could by going to bat for you. Please keep this confidential. We don't always give severance. In fact, we don't often give it unless it's a layoff or job elimination situation. But I could see you really were trying to get back on track. And your parents' health situation was out of your control and came at a really bad time."

When I open the envelope, I can't help but break into a grin. I didn't expect this much and it will go a long way toward making my life easier for the foreseeable future.

"Jean, this means so much. You're an amazing person and an amazing leader. Thank you."

"You're welcome, now to thank me, please go finish that transition plan."

"Will do!"

Chapter 34

For the next week, I work on wrapping up my 'old' job, bringing Charles up to speed, and starting to apply for new jobs. I still attend all the meetings with Charles and work to fill out the transition template. I feel like I'm being splintered into a thousand pieces. With so many priorities, it's hard to feel like I'm focusing on any one. Or doing a good job on them, more importantly. But I continue to try because I want to live up to my commitment to Jean. And I also don't want to be unemployed for long.

I get two interview requests out of my job search.

At least after this week, I'll have time to focus more fully on preparing for those interviews.

My first interview is in Leesburg, almost an hour away. I initially forgot copies of my resume I had printed and had to turn around, losing 20 minutes in the process. I felt flustered when I walked into the meeting room where the hiring manager was already waiting. Although they didn't mention anything about my timing, they seemed a tad bit annoyed at the beginning.

I explain why I was late to the meeting and hope the manager will consider it the exception rather than the rule. The conversation went well though, and I left with a good feeling that I'd hear back for at least a second interview.

My second interview is closer to home, literally, at the hospital where my dad had his surgery. I know the hiring manager for the hospital from high school.

Thankfully, I had my resume copies ready to go for the interview. I was able to answer all the questions with confidence and seemed to have built a good rapport by the end of the interview. I reflect on how I answered a few of the questions in a meandering way.

When asked to describe my style when I'm in a lead role, I talked about my experience at a food pantry where I volunteered…which made me think to explain how I got started with volunteering, which reminds me of my cat I had when I was younger…and so on and so on. At the time, the background seemed relevant and to the point. I hadn't actually held a role with the title of lead, so volunteering was the best example I could think of at the time. I sometimes coordinated the work of other volunteers. "Anyhoo, my style is flexible to the needs of the people I'm leading," I finally concluded.

Outside of the interviews, I enjoy the free time I have to catch up on work around my apartment, time with my parents, and my BFF, Amira. I decide to call Bryan and give him the scoop on my job situation, and maybe ask him out for another date. The jury is still out whether my relationship with Bryan will go any further, but I may as well at least give it a shot.

I call him and he answers on the second ring.

"Hey, stranger, long time no see."

He chuckles. "Yeah, sorry, I've been out birding my ass off.

"It's fall migration season now and I've been out looking for some of the unusual birds that come through here in the fall."

"Not a problem,I've been busy myself. I left my job and have started interviewing for new ones, so that's been a major time commitment."

"Oh wow, I'm not sure if I should say sorry to hear that or congratulations."

I'm not sure why I'm not telling Bryan the whole story of actually losing my job. I don't necessarily want it to become common knowledge in Lyndville and I don't know him well enough to know if he will keep the information confidential.

"I guess a little bit of both is in order. I don't think it was a good fit for my skills and style, so fingers crossed, my next job will be a better fit." My explanation is true yet vague.

"How about holding off on the congratulations until I find that next magical role that is perfect for me."

"OK, will do."

"So I was calling to see if you'd like to go out again. I have some free time on my hands. We could even go birding. It sounds interesting to me."

I'd like to go on a date that, presumably, won't involve drinking, just to get to know Bryan in a sober state.

"That would be great, Sophia. I'll take you over to Back Bay National Wildlife Refuge if you're up for a bit of a drive. It has a couple different environments for birding with the ocean and beach plus marshes by the bay. We might see something unusual like a Northern Lapwing, a Lesser Goldfinch, or an Ancient Murrelet."

"Well that's kinda mean, why do they call it a Lesser Goldfinch, lesser than what? And what do they call a baby Ancient Murrelet, they're not all old," I joke.

"The bird naming people usually just mean lesser to say they're smaller than something else that was already named or more common. So, a Lesser Goldfinch is about ½ inch shorter than an American Goldfinch, the ones we see commonly around here. They sometimes call something a 'greater' which probably gives them a superiority complex their whole lives."

I laugh. "I bet."

Bryan continues. "And the Ancient Murrelet is called that because of its gray back which is supposed to look like an old person's shawl. I bet you wanted to know all of that."

"It is pretty intriguing, in a bird nerdy kinda way. I'm betting they'll all look the same to me, but I know they're…what is it…taxonomically different so they had to come up with some different names. Not like they could call one X and the next Y and have that mean anything to someone trying to tell them apart."

"Right on, Sophia. You're gonna be a great birder. I can tell."

"Oh, and I was totally joking about the bird nerd comment."

"No offense taken, I actually wear my bird nerd label proudly, Sophia. In fact, I have a shirt that declares me so."

"That's awesome, you gotta wear that when we go out."

"You bet, what day were you thinking?"

"How does Wednesday work for you?"

"Sounds great, I'll pick you up at 6:30."

"Isn't that kind of late to go out birding?"

"I mean AM, not PM. Bird activity is best at dawn when it's quiet."

"Oh, right, ok. I'll set my alarm. See you Wednesday."

"See you Wednesday. And thanks for calling."

"My pleasure."

Chapter 35

Bryan arrives at my apartment right on time and is wearing his Bird Nerd shirt. He has binoculars for me to use and seems excited to share his hobby and passion with me. We have nearly an hour drive to get to the birding location, so we have time to catch up on the way.

"So what's new? How's your mom doing?"

"She's doing ok. She seems to have stumped the doctors though as far as what's going on. The allergy tests showed she's allergic to some common household things, but not extremely so. So it doesn't really explain the episodes. It seems like we're still just reacting to her breathing episodes and not really figuring out why they're happening. We may have to look for another facility that specializes in this sort of thing."

"How's your job hunt going?" Bryan asks, seeming to want to change the subject.

"We'll see, I guess. I had two interviews this week, and I don't feel like I knocked it out of the park, so to speak, in either. But I am hopeful I'll get at least one second interview. Lyndville is a great place but not a ton of jobs around here, so we'll see."

I leave out the part about being late to one of the interviews and rambling in the other. I stare out the window and enjoy the views of the sandy beach and lightening sky as we drive along the shore. Now it's my turn to change the subject.

"I've never used binoculars before, can you give me a quick overview, please?"

Bryan goes on to explain the use of binoculars. He tells me how to focus them and that it will actually help me see the birds' features and even their color better.

"Oh wow, what an amazing piece of equipment. I wish I had a pair of mind binoculars to improve my focus."

When we arrive at our first birding location, Bryan starts to explain that this is a hotspot according to an app called eBird.

"eBird is an amazing citizen science created app to gather data about birds from us bird nerds. It benefits all of us to know who is seeing what birds where. Long ago, this was done by word of mouth and even with a phone line, but now we can all do this in an app."

"As we go, I'll log the bird species we see and a rough count of how many. They use the data to understand if various bird populations are stable, on the rise, or on the decline. At times, a conservation group will step in to help."

"Red-headed Woodpeckers, for example, were a declining population and they figured out they could use golf course settings to re-establish the population. I read a whole study about it, really fascinating to me since it combines my passion for golfing and birding."

"I wondered about that tattoo on your forearm, is that a Red-headed Woodpecker?"

"Yes, I got that five years ago when I learned about the work."

"Cool!"

I take the opportunity to study Bryan's forearms, hands, and arms for a moment. He has a dusting of dark brown hair that glints in the morning sun. I'm thinking about how it would feel to have those arms wrapped around me when he says "You all ready to go?"

I tear my eyes away from his arms and my wandering thoughts.

"Yes, let's go."

Bryan explains the hobby of birding as they go.

"Our main goal with birding is to identify as many birds as we can. It sounds simple but it takes a lot of practice and accumulation of knowledge to be good at it. Sometimes we see the birds clearly but have to see some feature that's tiny or subtle, like a brown patch of feathers on their wings in order to identify them. A lot of times, we can't see colors clearly, or the bird flies away before we get a good look. And sometimes the birds are just too far away to get a good visual. Binoculars help a lot and some birders get scopes, which are even more powerful to see farther away."

"A lot of the time, our best way to identify a bird is by its call. We don't get a good look but we can learn the calls.

"That also helps us know what birds are around so we have a better sense of where to look. For example, there's a bird that migrates through this time of year called a Great-crested Flycatcher. Its call is pretty easy to learn and if I hear it, I know to look WAAAAAAAY up in the tops of nearby trees because it will probably be perched there."

"Holy cowbirds", I joke. I did a little research on common birds to get ready for the date and was looking forward to making that joke. But I feel a bit overwhelmed by all the information Bryan's throwing at me.

We spend the next two hours walking the shoreline of the beach and marshes with Bryan frequently stopping to check out a bird, log it in his eBird app, and tell me more about the birds he's seeing. I'm impressed by his knowledge.

He seems completely absorbed in the task at hand and I find I have plenty of time to study his strong calves, broad shoulders, and sinewy forearms as we go.

He occasionally puts his hand on my lower back or casually throws his arm around me as we walk, and I feel a zing of electricity. But he continues to be all birding business until we get back to the car.

He seems to shake himself out of his birding trance once we arrive in the parking lot. "I hope you had fun and didn't find this boring. As you can tell, I totally geek out on this stuff. I'm the same way with golfing. Don't get me started on that."

"It is interesting. A little overwhelming for me but that's not surprising for my first time. I have no idea how you can process when there are so many birds around. It was interesting." My mind wanders back to studying his handsome physique as we walked.

Bryan is now looking deeply into my eyes. His stormy blue eyes seem to look right into my thoughts. For a moment, we both forget we're standing in a parking lot. He dips his head and kisses me softly. Just as I think the kiss is going to get more intense, a bird calls nearby. Bryan pulls away suddenly and peers into his binoculars.

"I didn't mean to get carried away. I hope you don't mind."

"I didn't mind a bit."

"Well I have plenty more of those and next time, let's try kissing someplace other than a parking lot."

"Sounds good, I'll hold you to that promise."

Chapter 36

The next day, I hear back from the first place I interviewed in an email. I'm disappointed to get an email rather than a phone call but I remain hopeful.

"Thank you for your interest in our company. However, we've decided to pursue other candidates." My stomach drops. The email doesn't say anything else insightful about why I didn't get a second interview. I have to guess my tardiness was a factor, though. Showing up late to an important meeting never makes a good impression.

On Friday, I get a similar email from the hospital where I had also interviewed. "Blah, blah, blah, we regret to inform you." I decide to call my friend who works there and see if I can get any more feedback. Are there really good candidates I'm competing against? Did they close the position?"

"Hello, Susan? This is Sophia. How's it going?"

"Fine, thanks, Sophia, how about with you?"

"Pretty well, all things considered. Susan, I was wondering if you can do me a favor. Are you able to give me the real scoop on why I didn't get a second interview at the hospital? I really thought my skills are a good fit for the position."

"Sophia, I'm really not supposed to say anything more than the company line. But you're a friend so I'll give you a little more info if you PROMISE to keep it confidential."

"I promise."

"Well...when the hiring committee was comparing notes on your interview, the way you answered the leadership question really threw us. And it's not because you didn't have a ton of experience that way, it's because you went all over the place with your answer. I think you talked about cats? That didn't sit well with them."

My heart sinks. At that moment, I had really felt like my brain short circuited and I couldn't piece together my thoughts in a cohesive way. On some level, I knew that would be the answer, but I needed to hear it out loud.

I thank Susan for her candor and end the call. I wonder if that kind of brain cramp is consistent with ADHD and decide to call Ethan.

"Hey, Sophia, good to hear from you. What's up?"

I tell Ethan about getting two rejections and recounts my conversation with Susan about the meandering answer. I also fess up about being late for the first interview.

"So I was wondering, does that sound like I might have ADHD?"

"Oh Sophia, I'm so sorry to hear that. You're so talented and have great experience for those jobs. I'll start by saying I'm not qualified to actually answer your question. But as a close friend who does have ADHD I can tell you yes, being late and having difficulty telling a cohesive story are consistent with my symptoms anyway. At the same time, lots of people without neurodivergent tendencies can have the same thing happen. It would probably be a good idea for you to get a professional opinion."

"I know, Ethan and I appreciate it. I guess I was just looking for someone to help me justify the need to get tested. If you had said 'No way, nothing like my ADHD, I would probably have just moved on. But it sounds like you've had similar experiences."

"Yes, absolutely. And especially when I'm not taking my medications. The meds really help me with planning and focus. I love the practice where I go for therapy and where I was diagnosed. Would you like their contact info?"

"Yes, please, Ethan. Thanks as always for being such an amazing sounding board and support." I feel a rush of gratitude along with a warm tingle of heat from my call with Ethan.

"You're welcome, Sophia. Lemme know if there's anything I can do to help with your job search. I'll be your reference and write you a glowing recommendation."

"Thanks, Ethan, I may take you up on that."

Later that day, I contact Ethan's practice and ask to be tested for ADHD. I'm told they'll be sending me links for testing and that I'll need to ask other people to assess me as well. After all that is compiled, I'll meet with a professional who will have looked at all of the results and will give me the verdict.

In the next several days, I complete the online testing and ask my assessors to do the same. I'm surprised at how many steps the whole process takes. I wonder how many people just give up and don't get a diagnosis because their ADHD doesn't allow them to follow through. Maybe just completing all of this says I don't have ADHD, I think. The following Monday, I have an appointment with Dr. Oswell to hear the verdict.

After the opening pleasantries, Dr. Oswell gets down to business.

"Sophia, I'll cut to the chase. Your testing and the assessments others have done for you suggest you do have ADHD. Your recent issues at work and difficulties in getting your next job are also…how shall I say…indicative.

"A commonly held myth about people with ADHD is that they're not completing tasks because of a lack of motivation. And clearly, as you know, you're quite motivated. But your brain is different and gets off track more easily. Before we discuss a treatment plan, what questions do you have?"

I breathe deeply. I feel a little sad yet relieved. I didn't want to hear I have it, but it also explains so much in my life.

"I don't have many questions about the diagnosis, per se.

"I've done some reading and googling on my own. And my friend Ethan who referred me here has given me lots of information. I guess my only question is how it impacts my ability to work."

"Well, therapy can have a very positive impact, especially if you really start to make changes in your habits. And you'll likely find medication will improve your ability to focus.

"As well, your diagnosis will allow you to ask for what we call accommodations at work."

"What do you mean, accommodations?"

"For example, people with ADHD sometimes use noise canceling headphones or work from home from time to time so they have fewer distractions from the noise around them."

I think of the times Jean allowed me to work from home and how much more productive I was.

"Thank you, Dr. Oswell. I'll schedule behavioral therapy right away and start on the medication."

I feel hopeful for the improvements Dr. Oswell described as we wrap up the call.

Chapter 37

I follow through with an appointment for behavioral counseling, a prescription for a stimulant medication, and call Ethan.

"Hi, Ethan. How are you?"

"I'm great, Sophia. I want to tell you all about something that happened at the humane society this week...this one cat...wait, never mind. You called me. How are you?"

"You'll never believe what I learned this week. I have ADHD too. We can be ADHD buddies."

"Wow, that is news. And yet, not. I know you've been thinking you had it for a while. Although having ADHD kinda sucks a little, congratulations for finding out and taking steps to get better."

"Thanks. It definitely helps me understand what happened with my work situation, and I'm actually looking forward to starting therapy. I may be the only person to ever say that but it's true."

Ethan chuckles. "Yeah, it can be...how do I say...humbling at times to realize what an ass my ADHD makes me at times. I interrupt people, I'm late for meetings and appointments, I lose stuff. But rather than beating myself up for those things, I learn to put in place better systems to prevent them. I spent a lot of my life feeling like I was an asshole because I was always making people mad about something. But when I accepted it for what it is…my glitchy brain…and started working on the anti-asshole protocol, life got a lot better."

"That's great to hear. My first appointment is on Tuesday, I'll let you know how it goes."

"Yes, please do. Want to go out for lunch or drinks later in the week?"

"That would be great, ADHD buddy. Thursday? Take a look at your calendar and let me know if lunch or happy hour works better for you. Let's dig out that business plan, too, now that I have more time on my hands."

The appointment on Tuesday is a Zoom call. Dr. Oswell and I greet each other and jump right in.

"So Sophia, let's start with you telling me where and how you see ADHD impacting your life. Is it in relationships, at work? How does it affect you?"

"Well, I was recently fired from a job I actually liked. It's not like I wasn't trying to do a good job. But even when I had stuff due, I kept getting distracted. I was late for work sometimes for any number of reasons.

"My friend Ethan who has ADHD calls it his "brain glitches".

"My boss put me on a performance plan and was meeting with me regularly to work on it. But I wasn't able to keep up. I needed to be out ahead of the team to keep things running smoothly and I just couldn't."

I find myself wiping away a couple tears and I'm surprised to find how emotional I am about my work and letting down my teammates.

"Mmmmhmm. That makes complete sense and is not uncommon for people with ADHD. What else?"

"I guess this is along the same lines, but sometimes I start something around the house and then just get lost. So I'll literally be doing something like cleaning my bathroom and stop midway but forget I didn't finish it. I get a text and then four hours later, I find my gloves and toilet bowl cleaner just sitting there. I mean, that's not a big deal but because it happens all the time, it can kind of snowball.

"Like I forget I put laundry in the washing machine, find it the next day and it needs to be re-washed because it's musty.

"And then I don't have the shirt I wanted to wear for work that day."

"Sorry, I feel like I'm rambling."

Dr. Oswell chuckles. "Well, first of all, it's good you caught yourself with the rambling. A lot of people with ADHD wouldn't pick up on themselves rambling...it just sounds totally normal to them. And secondly, what you're describing at home is important and probably feels chaotic to you. I know you said it's not a big deal, but it's creating stress in your life, right?"

"Absolutely."

"So it's a big enough deal you want to work on it?"

"Definitely."

"OK, great. Tell me about how you plan your days and manage your time."

"Well, I used a calendar at work for meetings. And there was an automatic feature that told me a few minutes before the meeting that it was about to start. That helped some. but I could turn that off and still miss a meeting."

"Calendars and reminders are a great start. What about your personal obligations? How do you manage that?"

"I keep most of that in my head. And when I was working full time, I didn't have a ton going on outside of the job anyway."

Dr. Oswell studies me for a moment through the screen. "At the risk of sounding glib, how's that working out for you?"

I laugh. "OK, I guess, but maybe not considering my toilet bowl example."

"Right, a lot of my patients find using calendars, reminders, and planners more…I'll say holistically it is very helpful. By that I mean having their work and personal calendars integrated so they can see all of their commitments and avoid overscheduling themselves. People with ADHD find that difficult, being realistic about how much time they need to do something. So having a visual of each day and blocking off the scheduled appointments and commitments helps us. And the reminders help us to not get lost in doing one thing on our list while losing track of another."

"Do you have a day planner you recommend?"

"Not really other than to say you'll want to decide if you prefer digital or physical or a little of both. Many of my patients find the physical calendar a bit daunting because they don't want to carry a binder around all the time. But there's also power in being able to write things down and check them off. It solidifies them in our brains. And this is important…checking something off our list gives us a shot of dopamine. Are you familiar with dopamine and ADHD?"

"Yes, Google and Ethan told me all about dopamine."

"Good. Some of my clients keep their calendars mostly digital to allow for mobility, like making a dentist appointment in the office without their planners. But they also keep their calendars up to date in their planner system. It's a little extra work but it seems to work well with the whole visualization need."

"How about for your next assignment, go out and do some planner shopping and bring back whatever you decide to try. And we'll talk about how you're feeling on your meds."

"OK, sounds like a plan. Get it? Planner? Plan? Thank you, Dr. Oswell."

"You're welcome, Sophia. I can tell you're motivated and that's going to make all the difference in tackling your ADHD."

"See you next week."

I call my parents and fill them in on the ADHD diagnosis. I tell them it's often hereditary so they may want to consider getting tested themselves.

Mom asks how I'm feeling about it.

"I feel really good, Mom. Before you start to feel sorry for me, it's one of the best things that has happened to me in a long time. I finally understand a lot of anxiety in my life. And I'm starting to do something about it rather than wallowing in it. I've started therapy with Dr. Oswell and he has me on a stimulant medication. Oh, and I'm trying to exercise more. Exercise seems to be the cure for everything."

Dad looks thoughtful and then smiles.

"That's great news, Sophia. Not the part about having ADHD but the part about feeling better. It would make a lot of sense if I have it too, thinking back to some of my job challenges. Your generation is so much smarter about mental health than our generation ever was.

Chapter 38

For the next couple weeks, I continue my therapy with Dr. Oswell and work to improve my planning and reminder system. I continue to look for job prospects, but I find my heart isn't really in it. I think the universe is giving me a sign to pursue my dream of opening the coffee shop. I don't want to look regretfully at the doors that have closed, I want to look at the doors that are opening.

I've also started borrowing "life hacks" from Ethan, such as using quotes to set the tone for a day. I find a quote I enjoy and that seems perfect for my day:

"There's a trick to a graceful exit. It begins with the vision to recognize when a job, a life stage, or a relationship is over-and let it go. It means leaving what's over without denying its validity or its past importance to our lives. It involves a sense of future, a belief that every exit line is an entry, that we are moving up rather than out." Ellen Goodman

The quote resonates relative to my job and my relationship status.

Perhaps with my ADHD, I'm not the best fit for corporate America where so much of the work is deadline driven. I can meet deadlines when I want to, but it's difficult for me. I'm also wondering if now is the time to make some decisions about my relationships with Bryan and Ethan.

Should I continue a relationship where the attraction seems largely physical without a significant emotional connection?

I decide to spend the next few days acting "as if" I'm going to open the coffee shop. I'll go out with Ethan and take the next steps with the business plan, loans, and grants. And I'll give Bryan another chance to see how it would feel to get more serious about the relationship.

Ethan and I agree to have lunch at the beach and talk about the coffee shop.

"Hey Coffee Queen, how's it going?"

I laugh, remembering our conversation about queen vs. princess.

"Thanks for getting together. I lost track of this with getting sick and everything going on at work but I'm ready to get serious now. You were working on cash flow projections, and I was working on marketing and customer profiles. Did you have a chance to put something together?"

"You bet. I had almost forgotten about it, it seems so long ago, but I put this together with some assumptions around loans and grants as the start-up money. I was going to drop it off that day you were sick. Check it out."

Ethan shares a spreadsheet that shows the startup in March, soft opening in April ,and full operation by the end of May. It includes a simple menu to start with to keep inventory and staffing levels low and maximize profits during the busy tourist season. That would also allow me to start repaying the loan quickly and spend less on interest payments.

"This looks great. Fantastic. And might I say, doable, Ethan. I think I can really make this happen if I can get the start-up money for these projects."

I share my marketing strategy and customer profile information.

"Obviously the main customers from late May through August are the tourists. I got some data from the Chamber of Commerce about how many people visit and projected how many would come to the coffee shop during the busy season.

"Then from September through the following spring, we would have the locals. I was thinking we would change the menu during that time. You know, offer the warm, pumpkin spice vibe in the fall. In winter, we would add items like a peppermint latte, hot chocolate, and other items to attract the locals. I don't actually think much marketing strategy is needed if we get the right things on the menu. This stuff will sell itself."

Ethan is staring at me. My excitement is bubbling up and is that a flush I feel in my cheeks? He raises a hand gently toward my flushed cheek and leans toward me. It's making me think he may be about to kiss me. But suddenly he stops himself and seems to go back to business mode.

"What do you think, Ethan? You had a funny look on your face."

"That all makes sense, Sophia. It won't take long for the locals to find this place since we have such a coffee desert here, so marketing won't be a huge expense. You'll be an oasis in the desert. I see you included some events early on to get the word out and a Facebook page. I can use the customer visit projections to refine my revenue projections."

"Sounds good. Make that spreadsheet magic work. Now, let's talk about location. I was thinking I'll buy a food truck to start and then rent an indoor space in the colder months to save money until we can figure out if it makes sense to actually open a shop. What do you think about that idea?"

"I like it. I like it a lot because it minimizes expenses in the start up year. The people at the bank will like it too, I think.

"It minimizes the risk of you not paying them back."

"Yep, that can get plugged into this magical spreadsheet, too. So since I'm the Coffee Queen, you can be the Spreadsheet King."

Ethan grimaces then smirks.

"Somehow that doesn't have the same ring. I'd take Espresso King or Latte King, but Spreadsheet King? That sounds nerdy."

"Nerdy is hot, don't knock it. Have you seen those TikToks?

"I'm looking for a man in finance, trust fund, 6 '5, blue eyes," I say in a sing song voice.

Ethan smiles and takes a deep breath as though bolstering his courage.

"So how would you feel about going on a date with a guy in finance? I am close to 6 '5, no trust fund, but I'll buy you dinner. Are you free on Saturday?"

I think for a moment about my earlier train of thought about Bryan. I decide to have a "date off" in the next few days and make a decision if I want to get more serious with Ethan or Bryan.

"Sounds great, see you Saturday."

Chapter 39

I have another session with Dr. Oswell that week and decide to pick his brain about my relationship status. It seems a bit off topic, and yet not, since I recall reading that ADHD can impact relationships.

"Good morning, Sophia. I believe we said you were going to do some planner shopping this week, and we can continue discussing where and how you're seeing ADHD impact your life. And then we can discuss tools and coping mechanisms for what's impacting you the most."

"Yes, well, I did some planner shopping, but I didn't find anything that I think is going to work for me."

Dr. Oswell looks slightly surprised.

"Go on, what's lacking in what you found?"

"Well, a lot of them don't have enough space for me to write everything down that I have to do in a given day. And then some days are more structured than others. I don't want an hour by hour breakdown on weekend days, but I do want that during the week. And my friend Ethan suggested using quotes each day to get in the right frame of mind. I'd like an area to put a quote of the day. That will help me with managing emotions, like if I have a day I need to focus on forgiving someone."

"Those are valid points, Sophia. I'll tell you what. I have a template I can give you that you can customize to your liking. It has a schedule section, plenty of room for your to-do list, and you can add the section for quotes easily. I think this is going to be such a helpful tool for managing your ADHD, I don't want you to put off getting started.

"Procrastination can be a challenge for people with ADHD, whether it's because you want to make something perfect or just getting distracted by something more fun and interesting."

"OK, I'll give it a try, I promise. No more procrastinating."

"So what are you finding to be most impactful about ADHD in your life now?"

"Well, I don't know if this would be an ADHD thing, but I'm trying to decide between a couple of guys. Do tell me if this is too off topic, but one of the guys has ADHD, one doesn't, as far as I know. Without getting into a ton of detail, the one with ADHD I consider a close friend and feel emotionally connected to him. The other one I feel a strong physical attraction to, but not as much on the emotional support side."

"I can tell you about the impact of ADHD on relationships which may help you watch for your own behavior and what to be careful of with the gentleman who has ADHD.

"What's his name?"

"Ethan."

"OK. Well you, Sophia, with your ADHD and Ethan with his may have a tendency to talk over one another and have difficulty listening and processing what each other is saying. Either or both of you might find it difficult to pay attention or forget appointments, which can lead to resentment and frustration. Either of you could end up feeling unheard or ignored. Even if you are very much in love, you and he could be so distracted by the phone, the TV, or internal thoughts, it could be difficult to see and feel that love."

"Wow, that sounds like a recipe for a relationship disaster."

"It certainly can be. But just like we are talking here about strategies you can use to manage your ADHD based on what's impacting you most, you can do the same for a relationship. If, for example, Ethan tends to hyperfocus on something like online gaming, you could ask him to set an alarm and suggest he get up and move around when the time is up to get his mind out of whatever it was he was hyperfocused on."

"Makes sense. Anything else?"

"We could spend a whole hour on relationship impacts if you have specific concerns to discuss, but it sounds like right now you're just trying to decide whether it's a good or a bad idea to have a relationship with someone who has ADHD.

"The simple answer is while it could create its own challenges and issues, there's no reason to avoid it especially since you would be going into it with solid knowledge of what to watch for. Also, it could be helpful for the two of you to "share notes", so to speak, about what's working well for you and what's not. Also I heard you say something super important. You said Ethan is emotionally supportive, so that tells me Ethan is doing a decent job of listening and not getting distracted."

"Yes that's true."

"So if he wasn't great at it before, he's gotten better."

"Good point."

"So the other guy, what's his name?"

"Bryan, he's new in town. He's here because his mom's health is not great."

"I see, so no ADHD as far as we know. I guess I would just suggest that when you think the time is right, you tell Bryan about your ADHD so he is going in with that knowledge."

"Another good point."

"What other major impacts are you finding with your ADHD?"

"Losing stuff! I can't tell you the number of times I'm rushing around my apartment looking for something I swear I put down in one place and it's not there."

"Yes, losing things is a common symptom. Some of the tips my patients find helpful are putting things in the same place all the time. If it's keys you tend to lose, get yourself a key hook to hang on the wall and hang them up every time in that same place. Some of my patients also use bright colors so they can easily spot, for example, their neon pink phone case anywhere in the room. And some patients use trackers for important items. You've probably seen them used. It's a small device that you can send a signal to and it makes a noise so it's easier to find. And finally, just be mindful of when you're setting something down. If you tell yourself I'm putting my keys in my pocket now since I'm not near the hook, you can solidify that in your memory when it's time to find them."

"Those are all great suggestions, Dr. Oswell. I'll get started with the planner template and try out some of these strategies to avoid losing things. Thanks,"

"You're welcome, see you next time, Sophia."

Chapter 40

I start using the template Dr. Oswell shared the next day. And on my to-do list, I include calling Bryan to ask him out. I'm committed to making a decision between Bryan and Ethan in the next week or so.

Bryan picks up on the third ring.

"Hey, Sophia, good to hear from you. What's new?"

My ADHD diagnosis jumps to mind but I decide I'm going to wait and tell him about when we're face to face.

"Oh, you know, keeping my parents out of trouble, taking care of the apartment, usual stuff. How about you?"

"Usual stuff for me too. Birding, golfing, and keeping an eye on my parents. They're doing pretty well, all things considered. I'm also checking in with my work. I'm on family medical leave now and I don't want to lose that job."

"Ah, I didn't realize that, it makes sense."

I screw up my courage and say, "Would you like to have dinner on Friday?"

"Sure, that would be great! Where would you like to go and what time?"

"Are you tired of Moma's? I just love their small plates."

"Not at all. I think we can find some new things on the menu and order our favorites again. Pick you up at 5:45?"

"How about I pick you up?" I think about the time we needed to Uber after Bryan had a few too many drinks.

"Sure, that works, see you then."

Friday afternoon, I invite Amira over for a late lunch and pre-date preparations. We have fun doing my makeup and hair in a date ready style. This time, I go with soft waves for my deep brown hair. Amira chooses a shimmery eyeshadow that highlights the gold flecks in my light brown eyes. I dress casually, but flirty, with a flowing flowered skirt and tank top that shows just enough cleavage to draw attention.

"How are you going to decide between Bryan and Ethan, Sophia? They're both hotties, if I'm being honest.

"Whoever you ditch, I'll take," Amira jokes.

"I have to go with my gut. They are both nice looking, but of course, that only goes so far in a relationship. I'm going to pay attention to the level of sparkishness I feel with each of them. And that is physical but also emotional.

"I need to have a sense of intimacy with a guy to have strong sexual feelings for him."

"Sparkishness? Is that the word for the combination of physical and emotional attraction then?"

"Yes, that's my new word for it. I'll report back to you on the sparkishness score of each of them on a scale of one to ten."

"I can't wait to hear! I'm working tonight so I'll be spying on you. Now let's get you some cute jewelry and you're ready for the first sparkishness test."

I pick Bryan up at 5:45. He looks handsome as ever in a tailored yet casual gray shirt that brings out the stormy color of his eyes. He's wearing shorts that give me a nice view of his strongly muscled thighs and calves as he gets into her car.

When we arrive at Moma's, we choose two new items from the tapas menu. We start with a charcuterie board with local cheeses, tangy olives, and crusty bread along with poblano peppers stuffed with a creamy cheese and herb blend. I choose a non-alcoholic beer and Bryan orders a margarita. We continue to catch up while we wait for our food and drinks.

"So, I never asked you about your job. Where do you work? Or were you working back in Pittsburgh?"

"I work for PPG. That stands for Pittsburgh Plate Glass Company. I work in their Human Resources department.

"Over fifty thousand employees work for PPG so we keep pretty busy in HR."

"I'll bet. So how long are you on leave from there?"

"I can take up to twelve weeks on FMLA, Family Medical Leave Act, and still keep my job."

"And remind me, how long have you been here in Lyndville?"

"I've been here six months going on seven."

Our drinks and first course of food arrive. Bryan asks the waiter for another margarita when he has a chance.

We continue to catch up and enjoy the tasty tapas.

Our second round of food includes the burger sliders and a crunchy wedge salad we had on our last date. And Bryan orders his third margarita.

Amira stops by their table to say hi. I introduce them and she gives his hand a firm shake.

"So nice to meet you, Bryan. Sophia's told me all about you."

"Oh really? There'shh not much to tell. Other than I'm hot. And you know...you are too...hot. Hot to trot I bet." All of this comes out sounding more than a little slurred.

Amira shoots me a look, picking up on his tipsiness and inappropriate comments.

"So your mom is doing better?"

"Yeah, she's improved with the breathing treatmentsh," he slurs. "I may be going back to Pittsburgh soon."

I consider what he's saying, and I realize I don't want a long distance relationship. And he's shown me his drinking seems to be a consistent pattern, at least right now. I initially thought maybe he was drinking to ease the stress of his mom's medical difficulties. But even now that she's better, he's still three drinks in after only an hour of our date. Not to mention, he's acting like a jerk with his comments to Amira. I'm very glad I'm the one driving.

I'm a little disappointed thinking back to the crush I've had on Bryan and how I fantasized and romanticized our relationship. But I'm also relieved because he's made my decision easy. He's going to likely be gone soon. And I've read about being in a relationship with someone who drinks too much. They're often emotionally unavailable, so he would likely never get a sparkishness score above a five in my book.

After listening to the band for an hour and Bryan ordering another margarita, I decide to call it.

"Are you ready to head out? I have a busy weekend."

"Awww, you're a party pooper? I wazzh jist getting ready to ashk you to dance."

"I'm totally a party pooper, let's head out."

I don't get out of the car when I drop Bryan off at his apartment. I realize his departure and his drinking are the last straws for this relationship.

"Bryan, I don't think we should see each other anymore.

"You're heading back to Pittsburgh soon, and I don't want to do the long distance thing. I need a level of intimacy in a relationship that I don't think our relationship can accommodate, especially long distance."

"Also, have you ever considered you may have an issue with alcohol? I don't know you well but it seems to me you drink more than most people. You might think about dialing that back or getting help if you can't on your own.

Bryan's eyes are slightly unfocused and he looks disappointed.

"I get it, Sophia. I get little tipsy shometimes but I'm sure I could quit anytime. You're a wonderful pershon and I wish you the besht."

We hug briefly and Bryan stumbles into his apartment alone.

I text Amira when I get home.

"Guess what."

"I think I can guess but tell me. He got a negative one on the sparkishness scale."

"For sure. I didn't include negatives on the scale, but Bryan may call for that. I broke it off with him. He's probably moving back to Pittsburgh anyway so that gave me an easy out.

"You saw how tipsy he was, and it wasn't the first time. That was really creeping me out. And his comments to you…I just had enough."

"Good for you, Sophia. If Bryan really does have an issue with alcohol, he would probably avoid commitment, get defensive, and lack empathy. You don't need that sh*t in your life."

"No, Amira, I don't. I deserve better."

Chapter 41

On Saturday, I check out the template Dr. Oswell gave me as well as the one from Ethan which includes the quotes section. I do believe the quotes will be helpful for managing emotions. I read up on how ADHD impacts emotional regulation. One article I read suggests a part of the brain in people with ADHD is underactive, resulting in emotions taking over rather than thinking things through rationally. Another article suggests low levels of dopamine can have the same effect.

So basically, where someone without ADHD can effectively calm anger or not overreact to criticism, a person with ADHD can tend to let those negative emotions take over their day.

Oh, *lovely,* I think sarcastically. But I consider how the use of quotes and my planning tools would help. For example, last Wednesday, I got angry with my dad for forgetting to give me some contact information. Then I recall a quote I found from Joyce Brothers that goes, *"You need to give yourself permission to be human."*

Obviously my dad didn't intentionally neglect to track down the contact information.

And in fact, I'm pretty sure my mom and dad also have ADHD, so all the more reason to be understanding of his humanness. The quote helped me work through the emotion, and I jotted a to-do to check into the contact I needed.

I also read about what can increase dopamine levels, since many articles point to low dopamine in individuals with ADHD. Not surprisingly, exercise and sleep top the list. I haven't been exercising regularly, and in fact, I get overwhelmed even thinking about adding that to what feels like an already long list of to-dos. I decide to talk with Dr. Oswell about it in my next session. The sleep articles point to the fact that dopamine levels are highest in the morning and drop throughout the day. So tackling difficult things in the morning will be a good strategy.

Going to bed and waking at the same time every day are also suggested. I decide I can take that one on as a trial and see how it goes. I've not been paying attention to my bedtime and will tend to vary it by several hours during a given week.

Another article points to music as a way to increase dopamine levels. Therapeutic benefits can come from listening, singing along, and dancing to upbeat and/or calming music. I'm again hesitant to add more to my to-do list, but I could easily listen to music at specific times throughout the day, like when I'm driving or doing chores around the house. I decide to give that one a try too.

All of this is well and good, but I also need to figure out how I'm going to make a living if I don't do the coffee shop thing. I continue to feel uninspired by going back into a corporate job.

Heading to a noisy office building, constantly being pressured to meet deadlines, and having frequent distractions to manage sends a shiver up my spine. I don't think I'm cut out for that, at least not right now with where I am in learning to manage my ADHD.

So I recommit to putting my time and energy into the coffee shop plan. I'll talk with Ethan about it a bit, although tonight will be more date and less shop talk.

Ethan is picking me up at 5:30 and we plan to go to the Mediterranean restaurant and then for a walk on the beach. The weather is perfect today, mid seventies and low humidity. I turn on a calming jazz playlist and dress in a casual blue and white striped sundress and light makeup. A swipe of mascara, some strategically placed shimmer on my cheeks and eyelids and I'm almost ready. I style my wavy brown hair into a loose coil on the top of my head and feel naturally pretty. As I look in the mirror, I see a sparkle in my eyes and a natural glow to my complexion that I had been missing in the last few months when I was dealing with so much stress.

"Wow, you look amazing." Ethan says when he arrives.

"Thank you, I have ADHD to thank," I joke.

"What do you mean?" Ethan looks confused.

"I'll tell you all about what I'm learning and doing to manage my ADHD while we drive."

I describe my sessions with Dr. Oswell, listening to music, and using my planning template.

"Getting fired may have been the best thing that's ever happened to me. I'm starting to feel so much better, so much more in control of my thinking and my destiny."

Ethan smiles broadly.

"That's so fantastic, Sophia. I felt a similar increase in my happiness when I started dealing with my ADHD. Rather than feeling overwhelmed all the time, like I was failing and letting people down, I started to focus on making improvements where it mattered. I started to catch myself when I was interrupting people and releasing my excess energy by exercising. Those things alone made a giant difference in my life."

We arrive at the restaurant and place our orders. I choose a platter with Greek orzo salad bursting with parsley, fresh lemon, and veggies and an order of spicy falafel. Ethan orders a shawarma chicken with warm pita and hummus dip. We each get a Greek coffee. Ethan orders a traditional hot, strong, and bitter coffee with a creamy foam on top and I order a frappe, a cold Greek coffee with milk and sugar.

We walk along the sandy beach to a spot with wooden picnic tables and enjoy our delicious meals and coffees while watching the waves. I use this quiet time to reflect on my

feelings for Ethan and sneak glances at his fit physique. He has
started to be more than a friend in my mind. His 'boy next
door' looks and charm are relaxed and relaxing, I realize. I feel
serene with a buzz of electricity when I'm with Ethan. He
understands me so well. And to be understood is one of the
greatest longings of my heart.

After dinner, we talk briefly about the coffee shop process.

I plan to apply for loans and grants by the end of the month.
I'll ask Ethan to help only if I get overwhelmed. I want to do
this on my own. All of the paperwork and boxes I need to
check may paralyze my brain briefly, but I know if I take it a
small chunk at a time, I'll get through it.

When Ethan drops me off that night, we share our first kiss.
Time seems to slow down. I feel nervous anticipation and the
closeness of Ethan's body radiating warmth. As our lips meet for
the first time, there's a spark—a rush of adrenaline and emotion.
The world fades away as every sense becomes heightened: the
softness of lips, the rhythm of breath, and the pounding of
hearts in sync. It's tender yet intense, filled with the unspoken
desire and curiosity of exploring something deeply intimate.
Each movement feels like a delicate balance between urgency
and savoring every second, a perfect blend of connection and
longing.

I stare deeply into Ethan's green gray eyes afterward, feeling
as though we can see one another like no one else can.

"This night has been fantastic. Can I take you out to lunch on Wednesday?"

"This night has been more than fantastic and yes, I would love that."

Chapter 42

I find myself energized by thoughts of Ethan and the coffee shop dream. I use this extra energy to work on the application for a grant, a loan, and figuring out the financial side of the coffee shop business.

I'm working on the spreadsheet that Ethan started but finding that I'm frustrated by the complexity and formulas.

And I feel like I may be rambling with how I'm filling out the grant application. I'm probably providing too much information about why I need the grant from a personal standpoint, and I should focus on the business side.

I decide to step away for a bit and go visit Amira. And I decide I'll walk to Amira's for some exercise. Kill two birds with one stone, so to speak. What an awful saying...Bryan would not approve.

Amira and I catch up on the balcony of her apartment over a cup of coffee.

"Tell me all about your date with Ethan!"

"I have to be honest, once I broke it off with Bryan, it really freed up my head...and my heart, I guess, for what I'm feeling for Ethan. He's genuine, he's warm...well, actually he's hot! And I just hadn't been thinking of him that way before."

"Where did you go? What did you do?"

I tell Amira about our Mediterranean meal and stroll on the beach.

"OK, now for the good part, did he make a move?"

I laugh. "That sounds totally high school but I guess so, we had our first kiss. And not to sound all rom com on you, but it was magical. Like kissing someone you not only find physically attractive but you share an emotional connection…that takes it to a whole nother level. I don't know if I can put it into words very well."

"You just did, I get it. At least from all the rom coms I read, I get it. I haven't been lucky enough to make that kind of connection in my dating scene yet, but I can picture it. And someday, I hope I will."

"I know you will, Amira. You're an amazing person and you'll find the right person. Give yourself a break. You just got back from your France trip. And it's not like you were going to start a relationship before or during that trip. But now you're here for the foreseeable future so…Mr. or Ms. Right is probably around the corner."

"Maybe so. Right now, I'm happy to be single, and honestly, getting to know myself better. And they say that's often the best time to find someone is when you're not even looking.

"I love the quote by Mark Nepo about *'The flower doesn't dream of the bee. The flower blooms and the bee comes.'* That's where I am right now."

"That's perfect, Amira. That quote is beautiful too, I'm totally stealing it for myself and Ethan. Once I started to bloom, Ethan the bee found me."

Amira cracks up. "Feel free; steal away. So what's up with your job situation?"

I blow out a long breath.

"I haven't given up entirely on a job search, but I have to say my heart isn't really in it. Corporate life is all about deadlines, and my ADHD makes it really hard for me to hit deadlines.

"Not impossible, but definitely more difficult than for people without ADHD. So I'm seriously thinking about giving the coffee shop a go. I've been working on applications for a grant and a loan."

"That's awesome, Sophia. How's that going?"

"Ugggghhh, kinda overwhelming at the moment. Ethan gave me a good start on a spreadsheet, but I think I'm breaking it. All those formulas and cells to fill out make me nuts."

"Have you asked for Ethan's help?"

"I probably will, although he's done so much already. I don't want to bug him."

"Sophia, he's a whiz with that stuff. I don't think you'd be bugging him, I think he would enjoy it. Remember too, he's a bee...get it bug, bee."

"You're probably right. But I want to do this on my own to prove to myself I can do it."

"That's noble, Sophia, a good goal, but I know you and numbers aren't best buds."

"That's true. I actually felt like I was going cross eyed looking at that spreadsheet this morning. I feel better after a walk and talking to you. But it doesn't change the fact that I *cringe* just thinking about going back to work on it.

"Speaking of it, though, I should head home."

I walk back to my apartment and crack open the spreadsheet once more. I spend several hours that day trying to plug in numbers. But when I look at the results, I have broken formulas in some places and I get negative numbers where there should be positive numbers. I try going for another walk and when I come back to it, I don't have solutions. This just doesn't make any sense to me.

I finally text Ethan and ask for his help.

I send him a gif of a person banging their head against a keyboard. "This is me."

Ethan sends back an LOL emoji. "Calling now."

"How can I help? I don't want you or your laptop to be injured in the creation of this spreadsheet."

I explain my dilemma and what I've tried.

"I'm sure I can help, I kept a copy of the original spreadsheet so worst case, we start from that. Let's get together for lunch."

"I'll buy you lunch. How does Mexican sound? 12:15?"

"Sounds great, I'll see you then."

"Thank you so much, Ethan. You have no idea how much I appreciate this."

"It's no problem at all. I get to see you again, and you know I actually find this stuff fun. It's like a puzzle to solve."

"That's great you consider it a puzzle. I consider it a train wreck of epic proportions. See you at 12:15."

Chapter 43

When we meet at the restaurant, I feel that jolt of electricity when I see Ethan. How had I missed how cute he is, with that dimple that shows up when he smiles?

His eyes look extra green today, complemented by his sage green flannel button down.

We hug, share a brief kiss, and marvel at one another for a moment before sitting down.

"OK so tell me what's going on."

"Ugggggghhhh, I hate spreadsheets, that's what's going on. I tried to plug in the data where you showed me, but now there are errors in formulas or something. It's just not making any sense."

I show Ethan the data points I was entering. As I'm speaking, Ethan seems to be staring at my face. I know my nose scrunches up when I'm concentrating, so he's probably noticing that.

"Is there any hope?"

"Yes, pretty easy fix, I can see where the cells have lost formulas and that's hosing the whole thing. I can fix it this afternoon easily. Only if you scrunch your nose up cutely again like you were doing. I love your freckles by the way."

I punch his solid bicep and blow out a sigh of relief.

Ethan and I order our meals and enjoy a bowl of warm chips and fresh salsa while we wait. Ethan has a spinach, mushroom, and cheese quesadilla, and I have a spicy chicken salad bowl with corn and creamy black beans.

After we share our delicious meal, I get back to business.

"Before I messed this sucker up, it was actually looking pretty good. If I do the food truck thing for the first year to minimize expenses, I use a bit of my severance pay and get the loan and grants I'm applying for, I'll start turning a profit within a few months."

"That's what the grant committee and loan officials will want to hear. That's great, Sophia, congratulations!"

"I'm struggling some with the grant application part though. I feel like I'm rambling too much."

"I'm happy to read it Sophia, but my strength is in the numbers side of the house."

"OK, well give it a read and let me know what you think."

I wonder what it would be like to go into business with Ethan. He has such a strong head for the financials.

But at the same time, would working together damage our chance at a relationship? I decide to at least bring up the topic to see where his head is.

"So Ethan, I was thinking. You're so good at the financial stuff and you seem really into this whole coffee shop thing.

"What would you think of being my business partner someday? Probably not right away but after I get a solid start."

Ethan looks thoughtful.

"You know, Sophia, I am really into this coffee shop idea for our community and for you. And selfishly, I think if we were to go into business together, I'd get to spend more time with you. But I've also been thinking about the chance of a relationship with you. If we were in business together and starting a relationship, would that be a good idea? What if we got into a silly fight about...I don't know, paint colors for the kitchen walls or something like that?"

"Right, well we both KNOW the kitchen walls have to be tan, like a sand color to match the beach, but also because that would hide a little mess well."

"Exactly, Sophia. I know you're joking but that's the type of thing where you should be free to decide on your own and not feel like you have to share that decision with me. And besides, we both KNOW the kitchen walls should be teal to reflect the ocean vibe, so I KNOW you were kidding about tan."

"Touche. What you're saying makes sense, Ethan. I don't want to jeopardize a chance at a relationship with you, and I do want this project to be fully mine. I'm looking forward to being my own girl boss."

"Right on, you're gonna kick ass in this business. And I agree, let's consider it but maybe just not right away. Let's prioritize getting to know one another better." He waggles his eyebrows suggestively, making my skin tingle.

"That sounds good. Thanks for being honest and helping me think through that. You'll still be able to help me fix broken spreadsheets if I ask, though, right?"

"Absolutely, bring on your broken spreadsheets and I'll solve the puzzle. Now back to getting to know each other better. May I take you out this weekend? There's a great band at Moma's on Saturday."

"I'd love that. Thank you again for your help, I can't express my appreciation enough."

"You're welcome and I can't tell you how happy it makes me to see you so excited and happy! See you Saturday."

Later that day, Ethan sends over the repaired spreadsheet and his comments on the grant application essay. As he had said, the spreadsheet fix was quick and it seems back to working correctly. He doesn't have a lot to say on the grant application essay, just a few grammar and spelling edits to suggest.

The grant applications are due by the end of the week so I make those quick updates Ethan suggested and send it in. I also decide to submit my loan application that day. I haven't done a thorough review of the essay or the numbers with anyone else. But I decide they're good enough to go.

I'm very relieved to have checked those items off my to-do list and proud I was able to maintain the focus and momentum to complete them. Dr. Oswell will be proud, I think.

Chapter 44

Amira and I go out for brunch on Friday morning to catch up.

"What's on your agenda for this weekend, Sophia?" I'm doing a yoga and meditation workshop on Saturday morning. That's another thing we need in this town is our own yoga studio. I'm driving an hour away to get my ash-tanga kicked."

"What? What's ash-tanga?"

"It's a type of yoga that's super physical, a lot of challenging poses, pretty fast paced so you end up feeling like you get your ass kicked by the end of it. But it feels fantastic when you're done. Then there's a guided meditation that will encourage us to explore and release negative emotions. You know, the ones I bury and like to pretend they don't exist."

"Sounds awesome...ish...I guess."

"It's not for everyone, but it feels really good to me."

"That's great, Amira. You should think about opening a yoga studio here in Lyndville. You could even do beach yoga when it's nice."

"That would be super fun. That reminds me. How is your coffee shop stuff going?"

"Well, I finally submitted my application for the grant and the loan. To be honest, that part was absolutely awful. I struggled with the financial parts because spreadsheets hate me and I hate them. And just getting through all the parts sucked. If it wasn't for Ethan's help with the spreadsheet and just helping me plug through, I wouldn't be done."

"He's such a great guy, Sophia. I can't tell you how glad I am that you dumped Bryan and are dating Ethan. Ethan just seems like your soulmate somehow."

"It doesn't hurt that he truly understands me and my ADHD. Maybe that's what you're picking up on. Being with someone who knows my weaknesses and still likes me...that's empowering. So many times, I've gone into relationships trying to hide my flaws.

"But here I am with Ethan showing my true colors."

"And it doesn't hurt that he is totally H-O-T-T-O-to-go. When are you going out next?"

"Tomorrow, Moma's. Are you working?"

"Yes, I'll be cheering you on. I hope you get seated in my section so I can eavesdrop."

I chuckle. "Me too."

On Saturday, I go low key on makeup and hair. It seems fitting with the conversation I had on Friday with Amira. He likes me for who I am. I let my wavy hair air dry, put on a light gold eyeshadow that compliments my whiskey colored eyes, a swipe of mascara, and clear lip gloss. I pick out a cornflower blue sundress that shows off my toned arms and slightly sunkissed shoulders.

Ethan is right on time and smiles broadly when I open the door to my apartment.

"You look amazing," he says.

"You do too."

Ethan's olive button down is rolled up at the sleeves, showing his strong forearms. His shorts show off his muscular legs. I find myself daydreaming about our kiss and being held in those arms and pressed against those legs.

"Are you ready?"

I shake myself out of my daydream.

"Never been more ready. Let's go."

The meal at Moma's is wonderful. They have a few new specials on the menu featuring local seafood. Amira is our server and she explains the new items with enthusiasm.

"Everything is delicious but the specials today are amazing; fresh local seafood in all of them."

Ethan and I share a slightly spicy crab dip. We both choose a lemon pepper flounder with sides of asparagus and sage buttered wild rice.

After our meal, the band starts up. They start with slow dinner music, a saxophone leading the melody. The lights on the dance floor are low and candles flicker on the surrounding tables.

As Ethan and I step onto the dance floor, our eyes meet and linger, the unspoken desire hanging in the space between us. Our bodies move together in perfect sync, brushing against each other with the rhythm of the saxophone. Ethan's hand on the small of my back feels electrified and warming. We tease one another by moving closer together and slightly apart, increasing the excitement of the next touch. Our hips sway together, our chests nearly touch. Every motion feels like it's building up to something more, but we're both holding back just enough to keep the energy simmering.

Two dances later, we head out for a walk on the beach. The stars dazzle and the waves lap softly at the shoreline as we walk. We stop when we reach a private spot away from the view of the restaurant. Our eyes lock for a brief second, knowing what's about to happen but not needing any words. I step closer to Ethan, fully closing the space between us. Our lips meet in a fiery, urgent kiss – hungry as if we've been holding back for far too long. Ethan's hand tangles in my hair while his other hand grips my waist. Our hearts race and our breath mingles together.

The kiss deepens, becoming more intense – lips parting, breath quickening as we explore one another. Our movements are heated by tenderness, a mix of raw desire, and overwhelming connection. We melt into one another, losing track of time, wrapped up entirely in the heat of the moment.

After several minutes in the passionate embrace, we pause and breathe.

"Would you like to come over to my apartment?" I ask.

"I would love that."

When we get back to my apartment, we settle on the couch and pick up where we left off at the beach. The atmosphere is charged with desire, every touch and glance communicating a passion that has been building up for what feels like forever. Our lips reconnect, our hands grasp tighter and we pull each other close, our movements becoming more urgent. Everything around us fades, leaving only the heat of the moment.

★★

The next day, Sunday, I can't stop reliving the passionate scenes with Ethan on the beach and in my apartment. I feel a warm glow that continues to brighten my day. I can't help but compare my feelings with Ethan to how I felt with Bryan.

Ugh, I think that was so different and not in a good way. For me, true passion must come with a sense of emotional connection and that was lacking in my relationship with Bryan. I mentally wish Bryan well and look forward to my next date with Ethan.

I have dinner at my parents' house that night. I'm planning to tell them about my ADHD and my budding relationship with Ethan tonight.

"Sophia, what is going on with you? You look really healthy, glowing almost."

"

"Well, besides managing my ADHD, I have news. I've started dating Ethan and broke up with Bryan. I'm not sure why I only thought of Ethan as a friend before. We've gotten really close through this ADHD thing. He has it too, and he's been so helpful all along with helping me understand it and sharing his own experiences."

"Dating Ethan seems to suit you. I don't know if I've ever seen you looking happier and healthier."

"I look it because I feel it."

Chapter 45

Three days later, I get an email from the city about my grant application. I feel a tingle of anticipation when I see it. And yet I'm a little surprised because the decisions about the grants aren't supposed to happen for several more days.

"We regret to inform you…" I can't read further through my tears for several minutes. If I don't get the grant, the coffee shop will probably not be possible. Or it would put an immense amount of pressure on the loan portion of the funding.

I take a deep breath and read on.

"…your grant application is incomplete. As a result, you have been deferred for grant funds unless you resubmit a fully completed application by close of business on Friday."

I groan loudly and grit my teeth. I'm upset with myself for missing a section of the grant, but at the same time, there's still hope.

I re-open the grant application website and look for the section I missed. I'm supposed to outline the payroll commitments, including details about how often I'll pay my staff. I breathe a sigh of relief.

Although I'm not experienced in this area, it won't be too difficult to draft something up and have it turned back in by the end of the week.

On Thursday, I have another appointment with Dr. Oswell.

"Hello, Sophia. How are things going? What are you finding that is going well, and what do you want to continue to improve?"

This is a great way to start the conversation, get me thinking about the improvements I've made and keep the momentum with a commitment to what's next.

I've been using my planning template pages most days.

"Well, having a list of everything I want to get done each day is remarkably helpful. I really thought I could keep it all in my head but that's not actually the case. I sometimes totally forget important stuff or steps I need to do to get ready. And I can get super focused on something fun and convince myself I can spend hours on that super fun thing.

"But with my to-do list, I have a constant reminder of all the stuff I said I wanted to get done."

"That's great, Sophia. Having a visual guide of what needs to get done is very important for people with ADHD. Visual representations of a schedule and tasks help with staying on track and managing your time, as you've discovered.

"They're also helpful with breaking down tasks into manageable chunks."

"I can see how they would help. I've been working on a plan to open a coffee shop and was overwhelmed at the start with how to even get going. My friend, well my boyfriend…has ADHD and he helped me keep moving forward. I don't think I would have been able to do it alone."

"And keep in mind, Sophia, the template I gave you is one of many examples available. If you find something isn't working about it, find another template or customize your own."

"Gotcha. Yeah, I also sometimes find myself starting something that wasn't even on my to-do list for the day.

"Before, I probably would have just rolled with that, but now I bust myself doing it, and if it's important, I can reprioritize or put it on another day. So I still have those brain glitches but I'm a lot more aware of managing them."

"Don't be too hard on yourself either. You used the term "busted yourself" and that sounds a little harsh. Give yourself some grace and know it's just the ADHD brain talking. You sound like you're really doing great."

"Well, it's an uphill battle at times but I'm so much less stressed and anxious now than I was a month ago. I'm not in panic mode all the time. So having these successes helps me keep going."

"Fabulous, Sophia. What about what you'd like to keep working on?"

"Well, my precious little brain hiccups cause me to miss things. Just this past week, I had a really important deadline to turn in my grant application for the coffee shop. I did, which I was super proud of, but guess what, I missed a section. Thankfully I can still resubmit but WTF?

"Sorry for the language, I meant what the fiasco."

"That's not surprising, Sophia. You may want to use a double checklist method meaning you have everything on the list and then ask someone to do a quality review.

"Some patients with ADHD also have impulsivity, taking an action or saying something without thinking it through. That may be why you sent the application incomplete."

I laugh. "Funny thing about the double checking. I did ask someone to check my work, Ethan, but he has ADHD also so we both missed it. And I'll keep an eye out for the impulsivity. I guess I was moving too fast and submitted the application without doing a double check myself, so impulsivity *was* part of the problem. And I hear what you're saying, put a safeguard in place for a potential fiasco so I don't leave out something important."

"Exactly. I really do admire the work you're doing, Sophia.

"I'll send you a couple links you might find helpful. Keep up the good work and I'll see you next week."

Resources
Templates

https://clickup.com/blog/to-do-lists-for-adhd/

Strategies for Time Waste and Productivity

https://www.additudemag.com/adhd-at-work-time-wasters-and-productivity-killers/

Chapter 46

I commit to myself to make the updates to the application my top priority for the week. No getting lost in binge watching a new series, going to lunches, doing major apartment projects, and so on. I also decide to ask Amira to be my reviewer. I still want Ethan's feedback, but he may not be my best double checker.

Later that day,I receive an email from the bank on my loan application. Once again, I'm flooded with anticipation, anxiety, and a touch of dread to open it.

Dear Sophia,

We have reviewed your submission and are unable to approve the loan at this time…

Once again, tears spring up and blur my vision for several minutes. Maybe I shouldn't even bother with fixing the grant application. I can't afford to open the coffee shop unless I get both a grant and a loan.

I call Amira, sobbing.

"They turned me down…the bank…for the loan," I choke out through sobs.

"Oh Sophia, I'm so sorry. I'm coming over in 10 minutes."

Amira gives me a huge hug when she arrives 10 minutes later.

"Those assholes. They don't know what they're missing out on," Amira says.

"What was the problem with your application?"

"I'm not sure, I got too upset when I read the first line. I just called you right away."

"Well, I'm curious, let's take a look."

Amira cracks open my laptop and opens the email.

Her eyebrows raise in surprise.

"Sophia, they didn't flat out turn you down."

"Whaaaaaaaat?"

"They said they can't approve you now unless you get the grant money. And unless you provide a more concise essay on the plans for seasonality. Were you rambling again?" Amira jokes.

"Oh…my…gosh. I'm sure I was rambling again. So you're saying I have a chance?"

"Yes, Sophia, you definitely have a chance. They seem very interested in the business, and say they think it will be a good fit for Lyndville in the closing paragraph."

"Ah, well, I never made it that far."

"I'm sorry I made you come all the way over here for my meltdown crisis. Let me make you an espresso or a latte for your troubles."

"I don't mind coming over. I'm just glad this loan application still has a chance of working out. You know, I wouldn't mind working with you in this business once you get it up and going. I have good experience in the food service industry, and I have a good feeling this is going to turn out to be a success. Anyhow, I'm getting ahead of myself.

"Would you like help with finishing out what you need on these applications? I don't work until 5:00 tonight."

"Amira, that would be amazing. Ethan was a huge help with the numbers side of it, and he looked at my essay, but he even warned me that's not his cup of tea…or coffee I guess."

Amira and I spend the next several hours revising the essay and filling in what was missing on the grant application. We ask Ethan to do a final review on the payroll section to make sure it ties in with the numbers in the spreadsheet.

Just before Amira has to leave for work, I resubmit both my grant and my loan application. And now I wait.

At my next appointment with Dr. Oswell, I replay my emotional rollercoaster with the loan and grant applications.

"That sounds painful, but it sounds like you got through it, Sophia."

"Eventually, yes I did, with a little help from my friends."

"Well, a couple of things to consider, Sophia, as it relates to your ADHD. We talked last time about the tendency for people with ADHD to act impulsively, and it sounds like you learned that lesson in this case. I also heard you describe how you got very upset before you had even fully read the letter. Managing emotions can be difficult for those of us with ADHD. You likely have an overactive amygdala, a part of the brain that processes emotions. And you likely have an underactive prefrontal cortex, the part of your brain that filters and monitors emotions. So your response was more, I'll say, exaggerated than perhaps it needed to be."

"Yes, in hindsight, I can see that. So can I make a trade so my amygdala that's overactive can send its energy to my prefrontal cortex that's underactive?"

"Unfortunately, Sophia, we haven't figured out yet how to make that possible. We may try another medication if you find the emotional side of your ADHD to be problematic. A class of medications called SSRIs can be very helpful for emotional regulation."

"OK, well, I'll keep bringing you the updates on what seems to be most impactful for me with my ADHD, and we can keep tweaking how we manage the medication side. I think the stimulants have been super helpful for me for focus. I really don't think I could have muscled my way through applications for the coffee shop without them. It's a ton of details...many of them boring details, honestly, to me."

"Once again, Sophia, keep up the good work."

"Thank you, Dr. Oswell, I'll keep pushing my ADHD boulder up the hill."

"Great, have a good day."

The next week, I receive the news from the grant application that I've been approved! And two days later, after I report the grant approval to the bank, I receive approval for the loan. I can hardly believe my good fortune.

I call Ethan and ask him out to celebrate.

"CONGRATULATIONS, Sophia. I can't tell you how happy I am that this is going to happen. I know losing your job sucked, but talk about a door opening! How about I cook you dinner?"

"Wow, you are full of surprises. I didn't know you could cook."

"Well, I have a few special dishes I've perfected. I'm not a chef or anything."

I think back to my dream about Ethan as a chef…had I known he cooked and forgot? Perhaps.

"I make a really tasty palak paneer, it's an Indian spinach dish with cheese. How spicy do you like your food?"

"I liiiiiiiiike spicy," I say, hoping Ethan picks up on my double meaning.

"Well I'll make it medium hot and we can add more peppers if you still want it hotter."

"That sounds wonderful, I think this is going to be a hot night all around. I am soooooooooooooo excited about this news. And I literally have you to thank for so much of it."

"Not really, Sophia. I was just here to support you. You did it all."

"You're being humble, Ethan. You're the one who helped me get the ADHD diagnosis. And that led to me getting the help I needed to focus and finish all these applications. And I don't think I would have survived spreadsheet hell if it weren't for the magic you did at the end there."

Ethan looks thoughtful. "Well, I have to admit, Sophia. I had an ulterior motive. I've had a crush on you for like forever. So the whole coffee shop thing has been a wonderful excuse to spend time with you and get to know you better. And somewhere along the way, it just started to work out. I was a little worried you were interested in Bryan for a minute there."

Now it's my turn to look thoughtful. "I would call that an infatuation more than an interest. Bryan is a nice guy, but I can't say we clicked emotionally. And that's an important ingredient for me in a relationship."

"So…are you saying we do click emotionally?"

"That's exactly what I'm saying. And I also feel us clicking physically. I mean, I hope we are, I hope you're feeling the sparks I feel every time we kiss."

"Oh yes, sparks, flames, smoldering loins. Just like in those rom coms you love to read," Ethan teases.

I blush and feel that tingle of electricity warm my body.

"I can't wait to see you tonight for a spicy evening."

"Me too, Sophia, me too."

Acknowledgements

I'd like to profusely thank my amazing family, starting with my mom. She's a young woman in her eighties helping me edit a shared file in the cloud. How's that for showing the world *it's never too late to learn something new.* She's always noticed things that need fixing in my books, so what better way to put that talent to work. She says she enjoys doing it too so…win win!

Next, I'd like to thank my early readers of the book. Several of them joked that they may or may not finish the book, considering their own tendencies towards ADHD. They were probably not joking. But they gave me the general thumbs up that the story is interesting and does a reasonable job of depicting life with ADHD. Thanks to Eleni for giving me wonderful insights on the rom com angle of the story, Hannah for making me go deeper into Sophia's head, and Liz for author specific suggestions. In my second round of feedback, Cheryl gave me a very thorough set of final edits and perspective from someone without ADHD…like you're gonna wanna define it. Such excellent input, I appreciate all of you so much!

Thanks and kudos to Becky Dobbins, who was the designer and more for the Mindful Birding Seattle edition. She was enormously helpful in the reuse of the cover concepts and assets. Where my Adobe skills are lacking, Becky stepped in to show me how it's done and, in most cases, do the work.

My daughter, Hannah deserves the credit for the visual of the girl sitting by the beach with a pelican. She did that drawing many years ago, and I just recently unearthed it while doing some cleaning. We agreed it would work well for the cover and has a nostalgic aspect from our trips to the beach.

Renee and James Tee also had a major hand in the original cover design from color scheme to fonts to logos…all the things in which I suck.(Or don't choose to take the time to do.) They set it up in the original book, and it's too beautiful not to reuse.

And finally, I'd like to thank my cats who provided entertainment while I was slogging through the daily grind of writing, editing, formatting and all of the heavy lifting that goes into production of a book. They provided comic relief and levity for an otherwise serious topic.

Disclaimers

This is a work of fiction. Names, characters, places and events are the products of the author's imagination or are used fictitiously. Any resemblance to actual persons, living or dead, events, or locales is coincidental.

All references to ADHD are based on resources provided and summarized by the fictitious characters.